Garrett knew the instant Penny awoke.

Her body stiffened, and he was sure he'd frightened her with the intimacy of his presence. But when he drew back from her, Penny's hand clutched at his shirt. Her head tipped upward, and he looked down to meet her gaze. The firelight caught in her wide eyes, giving radiance to the emerald color. Her skin was sleep-flushed, looking soft as a fairy wing in the glow of the moon. She spoke her words in a quiet voice. The pull of them, however, was as strong as a locomotive.

"Stay, please. Just a little while longer."

The Marshal's
Pursuit

by

Micki Miller

The Marshal's Pursuit

Cover Art by *Rae Monet, Inc. Design*

The Wild Rose Press, Inc.
PO Box 708
Adams Basin, NY 14410-0708
Visit us at www.thewildrosepress.com

Publishing History
First Cactus Rose Edition, 2016
Print ISBN 978-1-5092-0998-9
Digital ISBN 978-1-5092-0999-6

Published in the United States of America

Dedication

Randy, you took care of business
so my mind could be free.
I love you always.

Chapter 1

Mill's Creek, Missouri 1880

An outlaw was robbing the bank!

Although she stood personally witnessing the abomination of her father's business, twenty-year-old Penny Wills could hardly believe it. These things happened in bigger towns, more lucrative towns, St. Louis, Kansas City, even Brighton. But here in Mill's Creek where every face was at the very least familiar? Well, it just didn't happen.

Penny cocked an ear and listened for movement from behind the counter where Neil, the young teller, fainted when the gun swung in his direction. She didn't hear so much as a sniff or a groan and worried Neil may have hit his head in the fall and suffered a serious injury. She considered asking the lone robber if she could tend to him, but when the foul-smelling man turned from the counter to the three other people in the bank, Penny stared into his cold, flat eyes and saw he held no mercy.

The grimy outlaw lacked the height and fine build of her father, Frank, who stood a few feet to her left, but he was taller than Bentley Werner, her father's starchy clerk, who was directly to her right and only a couple of inches taller than her five and a half feet. The robber's brown hair was likely shaded darker by the countless layers of filth, just like his long-lived jacket and trousers. Dirt caked his old boots in patchy layers. At his waist hung a sheathed knife, the wood handle with a nickel inlay surprisingly clean compared to the rest of him.

His eyes peered out between his ragged hat and the frayed and dusty red bandana tied around his face, dark as deep pits, narrowed, glinting with the power he held over his captives.

Penny clutched her beaded reticule tighter and rolled it into the folds of her lavender skirt. She'd only just collected her allowance from her father, and she didn't want this scoundrel to get his thieving hands on it.

"You!" the robber growled, stabbing the gun toward her father.

Penny gasped and moved to go to him, but Bentley grabbed her hard by the arm.

Penny raised her eyes to meet her father's. Her papa gave her a smile and a wink, instantly calming her. He glanced at Bentley then, stern meaning tight in his gaze. Bentley moved to stand in front of Penny. She bent her neck to peer around him.

"Easy," her father said to the robber. "I'll get the money for you." Frank then removed a burlap sack from a shelf behind the counter and opened the cash drawer. He spoke calmly to the outlaw as he filled it. "See, no trouble."

"Be sher you git all of it," said the robber. His voice sounded as dirt-clogged as his appearance, as if tiny stones rolled in his chest.

Bentley spotted her looking and again placed himself in front of her. For a few moments, all Penny could hear was a quiet rasping of bills and the jangle of coins. Glancing up at the back of Bentley's head, she caught him giving a quick and subtle nod. Was he sending a signal to her father, or maybe receiving one?

Peeking around Bentley, she caught only a brief glance at her father and the robber behind the counter before Bentley once more tucked her behind him. For almost a full minute or so, she heard nothing. They must have gone in the safe to get the money stored there.

At the sound of their footsteps, she moved on silent feet around Bentley. Her father walked to her side and turned around. He had his hands raised even though the man hadn't told him to do so. Her father looked at her again, gave her another smile, another wink, before facing the outlaw who held his gun in one hand and a burlap sack in the other. For the first time since she'd seen the rough man walk through the door, face covered, gun in hand, Penny knew some relief, for the ordeal was almost finished.

He must not have tied his bandana tight enough, for it hung loose at a slant, showing a bit of the left side of his face. He had a beard, the unkempt kind that grew from neglect rather than intent. It was scraggly, uneven, and looked as filthy as his hair.

"You got what you came for," Frank said in a calm, steady voice. "Now go on while you can, before somebody comes in, or sees you through that big window and gets the sheriff."

After shooting a brief look out the front window, where encroaching rainclouds dampened the sun-flow, the outlaw took a single step back. Then he took another. His boots made heavy thuds on the wood planks, and before he could catch it, the bandana slipped from his face and fell to the floor.

The right side of his face bore a thick scar, pale, raised, and running from an inch or so beneath his eye, slashing into his beard, forbidding hair to grow on its shallow mound. His thick lips twisted in an ugly grimace, baring brown and yellow stained teeth.

The outlaw turned a quick glance toward Bentley and Penny. A flicker of panic passed through his eyes, but it vanished in a single beat of her racing heart. His left hand brushed the hilt of his knife. He then pointed the gun directly at Frank, and before anyone could say a word, he pulled the trigger three times.

Penny screamed and ran to her father, falling beside him. She didn't hear the pounding footsteps of the outlaw as he ran from the bank. Bentley was speaking to her, but she couldn't hear anything over her own cries, couldn't see anything but three pools of blood growing on her father's chest, and the vacant stare of his eyes.

Chapter 2

Shelton, Missouri 1880

The late day sun surrendered its futile efforts to break through the ceiling of ill-omened clouds. Night was going to come early. Street dust hovered low, kicked up with the bustle of folks, most heading home for their supper, walking or on horseback, some in wagons filled with supplies and chattering children. More than a few men, ranch hands, drifters and such, headed for one of the saloons for a night of drinking, or gambling, or fancy women, maybe for all three. No one took notice of the two men riding toward the jail.

Marshal Garrett Kincaid pulled up on the reins of his sable stallion, but at this point, it was little more than a tug. His well-muscled horse was as tired as he was. Even the cold wind, too stubborn to give way to the imminence of spring, wasn't enough to revive him. Though he was only twenty-eight years old, today Garrett was so worn he could have been at least five decades older.

He glanced over to the horse tied to his, where his prisoner sat with his cuffed hands resting on the saddle horn. The Red Devil, the only name he'd been able to get out of him, named so by the newspapers for his numerous crimes of arson, looked just as tired after their long chase and the ride back. He was a slender, slicked-down man wearing a fine suit now marred with wrinkles and dirt. His waxed mustache had long wilted, and several coats of road dust now buried the shine of his shoes. For the first time in days, Garrett took notice of his own canvas duster. He looked no better.

Garrett dismounted and walked around to the criminal he'd hunted down for months, the man responsible for many thousands of dollars in damages, and far worse, the death of two people. Looking up at the bruised face of his prisoner, the marshal found himself wishing the man had put up more of a fight. Garrett yanked him from the saddle without regard for the hard fall.

"Sir!" the Devil shouted from the ground. A thin cloud of dirt swirled around him. "You've captured me already. You needn't be so rough."

"Needn't I?" Garrett mocked as he "helped" the Devil up by lifting the back of his shirt collar, causing him to gasp for air. "You *needn't* have set those fires costing businesses their livelihoods and good people their jobs. You *needn't* have burned any of the other structures you decided to torch, for that matter."

Garrett didn't touch on the deaths. He didn't trust himself to bring the miserable bastard in alive if he let his mind think on those two innocent people who woke up to find themselves trapped in a burning building.

"Only two were businesses, and it was after hours so no one was there. The rest of them were abandoned buildings. I was doing the towns a favor, getting rid of eyesores."

Garrett shoved him hard between the shoulder blades, propelling the Devil up the wooden steps and onto the board sidewalk. "One of them was occupied. A young couple died in the last fire you set."

"Squatters," the arsonist replied with disdain. "They were no one."

Garrett gave the Devil a good kick in the ass. It sent him flying through the partially opened door into the sheriff's office. The arsonist couldn't catch his balance and landed face down on the floor. Garrett walked in behind him, feeling a bit more revived.

Sheriff John Gladwin jumped up from behind his desk, his pen falling from his hand and smearing ink across the page on which he'd been working. He scowled at the mess and looked up again to see Marshal Kincaid walk through his door.

Glaring at his old friend, Garrett said, "Don't look at me like that, John. I'm cold, hungry, and tired. Besides, I brought you a special guest." He grabbed the Devil's collar again and yanked him up, once more making him momentarily struggle for breath.

"Sheriff," the Devil said when he could speak, his bound hands rubbing his throat. The chain linking his cuffs rattled slightly. "This man is a brute. I've been subjected to inhumane treatment since the moment we met."

Gladwin, a neat man even in his daily wear, five years older than Garrett and almost as big, looked over the new arrival. "Well, if it isn't the Red Devil himself. Look at that, you're flesh and blood after all."

Garrett didn't miss his friend taking note of the ugly bruise on the prisoner's jaw and the one beneath his still swollen eye.

Gladwin turned to Garret. "He does look a mite damaged."

"He falls down a lot." Had the Devil possessed the

powers of his namesake, the glare he shot Garrett would have burnt the marshal to a smoldering crisp. Garrett barely noticed, and he cared even less. He also ignored Sheriff Gladwin's raised eyebrow. "You got my wire, I take it."

"I did," answered Gladwin before turning back to look at the Devil. "And we got a real nice cell all ready for you."

Garrett fished a key from his pocket and unlocked the handcuffs. Sheriff Gladwin then escorted the Devil around the corner and down the hall to his cell. As the prisoner's complaints faded, Garrett stepped over to the potbellied stove in the corner and poured himself a tin cup full of coffee. Compared to his mother's special brew, it tasted like boiled soil. After the long, cold days and nights he'd just spent, though, the fact that it was hot and fresh elevated it to just a few notches below mediocre.

He leaned back against the wall where the stove had warmed the bricks, closed his eyes, and took another swallow. It tasted worse than the first. His hair had grown too long, and the curls that tended to form poked into his neck, irritating his skin till it matched his mood. He tipped his head forward and gave his neck a vigorous scratch, and then did the same for the growth on his face.

A moment later, the sheriff returned and poured himself a cup. He then rounded his desk, opened the bottom drawer, and removed a tall bottle of amber liquid.

"A little early to be dosing your coffee, isn't it?"

"It's for yours." Gladwin set down his cup and crossed the room. He opened the bottle and poured a splash of whiskey into Garrett's coffee before going back to his desk and returning the bottle to the drawer. The sheriff sat down, then motioned toward the chair on the other side of his desk.

Garrett pushed off from the wall and took the seat. He didn't know what the news was; only that he wasn't going to like it. "What?" he asked after taking a bracing sip. At least the coffee tasted better.

"A telegram came for you this morning."

"And?"

"There's been a bank robbery. Mill's Creek."

"Mill's Creek," the marshal said slowly, chewing on the name for a moment. "Yeah, I've passed through there a time or two. Nice little town. Pretty big news for a place like that."

"It gets bigger. Garrett, I know you tend to take these things personally, after what happened to your father and all." The sheriff paused and shot a longing glance at the drawer where he kept the whiskey.

"Out with it, John."

"The proprietor of the bank," the sheriff said as he shuffled through the orderly stack of papers on the corner of his desk. He found what he was looking for. "Frank Wills. He was killed in the robbery."

"Damn," Garrett whispered, closing his eyes for a moment. He knew all too well the depth of grief a murder left in its wake. Even after all these years, there were still moments when he struggled to keep his head above it. He scratched at his neck again.

"You're supposed to head down there first thing in the morning. You'll have time for a good night's sleep, a bath, and some barbering."

Garrett turned his gaze to the window. Droplets of

water had begun to fall. People dashed across the street this way and that trying to get to their destinations before the inevitable downpour.

"Maybe," John said, reading his friends thoughts, "the storm will have come and gone by then."

Garrett lifted his cup to his lips and tipped it, finishing the bolstered coffee to the last drop.

Chapter 3

A clap of thunder loud enough to rattle the windows caused the room full of somberly dressed people to jump. Several of the women gasped, clutching their tear-soaked linens to their chests. What had started as an early spring sprinkle halfway through the funeral turned into a downpour by the time the preacher said his final words. Nobody left early, though. And the growing storm didn't keep anyone from coming to the house after.

Huddled in her home with all those who came to pay their respects, the storm lashing at every wall and window, Penny could almost believe the Grim Reaper himself was pounding to get in, trying to claim what was left of her.

Soft murmurs of sympathy brushed by Penny like the waves of heat issued by the fireplace, neither quite touching. She couldn't imagine ever feeling comforted or warm again. Occasionally, someone would sit beside her and put an arm or both around her, and she wanted to garner solace from their efforts, but she was too numb to feel and too desolate to care. Her dear, sweet father, the last relative she had left, was dead.

Sitting on the green, tufted sofa in the front parlor of her home, Penny gathered up some of the good manners taught to her by Miss Priscilla during her time in Boston and at least met the eyes of her guests. It was a grand and taxing effort. They'd come for him, her papa, so she would do her best to graciously accept the kind things said about him and wait until they were gone before drowning in her tears.

Everybody loved her father. Most of the town had shown up for his funeral. Wet and cold, they flooded into the house now, she could see through the open double doors of the parlor where she sat, as if washed in by the storm.

She saw Pearl, willowy, and yet somehow sturdy, manage the influx of mourners with tireless grace. Pearl had been their housekeeper and cook since her mother died when Penny was seven years old. Pearl stood at the door offering towels to people from a stack on a nearby chair as soon as they walked in. Many handed over cloth-covered dishes, others brought jars of something they'd canned in the fall, all of which Pearl, or some other helpful soul, carried back to the kitchen. Before the door could close, someone else was coming through it.

No longer able to keep up the pretense of conversation, or knowing how or wanting to respond, Penny lowered her eyes. Mud splattered her dress. She brushed at it out of habit, not because she actually cared. The black crape was damp in places, soaked where the umbrella Pearl held over their heads offered little protection.

At a quick flash of light, brighter than the last, Penny shot a low glance toward the window. The storm beat against the house on spasmodic gusts of wind. Rain was coming down so hard she couldn't even see the clouds, just water snaking rivulets down the glass, mimicking the tears on so many of the faces around her.

Thunder boomed again, louder, closer. Still, more people arrived.

Snippets of conversation penetrated the bellows of the storm and murmur of low-spoken voices.

"Such a kind man."

"A lovely man."

"Active in the community."

"Charitable."

Every word was true. Not a single person had anything but praise for her father. He was a good man, pure and simple. The injustice of his death was maddening.

And then, in the quiet of her immediate surroundings, as no one was now speaking to her directly, Penny picked up varying versions of "Whatever will happen to her now?" Some of the voices were sympathetic, cushioned with heartfelt concern. Other comments bore an edge that felt honed.

Subtly, she cocked her head, listening to what she could hear between offers of sympathy and the blows of the storm. What she heard in those hushed conversations, surely not meant to reach her ears, left her equally ashamed and surprised. Did these people who she'd known all of her life really think her so helpless? For that matter, Penny considered after some raw thoughts had their way with her, were they even wrong?

Papa had taken good care of her. That was certainly true. She supposed he also over-indulged her a bit. Well, more than a bit. After her many shopping trips to Kansas City, she had far more clothes than she actually needed. The spare room hosted her bounty. Her collection of bonnets was so grand they required a cabinet all their own. Papa found that amusing, as he did all her extravagances. It never failed to make him smile whenever she flounced downstairs to show off some new item for him.

She'd gone to a wonderful finishing school in Boston. She was the only girl in town afforded such a luxury. Her father's reasoning was sound. He simply wanted her to learn all of the refined skills of being a lady since she had no mother to teach her. He always worried and fussed about making up for what she didn't have.

There were times when Pearl made an effort to dissuade her from adding to her collection of frills. Pearl said it showed her in an unfair light, that others might be envious, some downright jealous. But she liked the nice things Papa so enjoyed buying. However, it was possible Pearl's argument held some validity.

Her papa was good to her, certainly, but he hadn't disabled her. He never allowed her to behave in an unladylike way. He saw to Penny's manners and raised her to think of others, made sure she was involved in many of his charitable endeavors. From the bits and pieces Penny picked up every time the storm took a breath, well, they were making it sound as if she couldn't so much as lift a spoon to her mouth without her father there to assist her.

It was true that anytime she had a problem, he handled it for her. He took care of everything. It wasn't that she couldn't do for herself. He just, well, it was so easy to let him handle things, and it made him feel good to do for her. It assuaged the guilt he carried for having raised her without a mother. Their lifestyle worked well for both of them.

Papa hadn't pushed her too hard to marry, even though most of her friends had already. Clarisse, her closest friend, had given birth to her first child shortly before Christmas. Penny had to admit, when she held Clarisse's baby girl something tugged her toward adulthood. She glanced to where Clarisse sat across the room holding her tiny daughter while others fussed over the sweet little thing. Maybe someday soon she would be ready.

It wasn't as if she didn't have suitors. Every time there was a dance, some young man, if not several, asked her to go. If there was any serious courting, however, she shunned it and them. None of them flared her interest. They didn't give her a lasting fascination. They weren't like the heroes in some of the dime novels she liked to read in between the more thought-provoking tomes. Besides, she saw no point in rushing into marriage. Her life was happy and full. For the time being, she was perfectly content spending her days reading books, tending her wardrobe, giving tea parties, living her life just the way it was.

Or rather, the way it had been.

The storm eased up a bit, though the respite lasted less than a minute. It was long enough to give Celia Carter, who along with her husband Jeb ran the mercantile, enough time to reaffirm her reputation as the town busybody. Celia's voice cut through the brief lull and wedged deep into Penny's consciousness.

"Penny might be well off to go live in a convent," Celia said. "It would do her good to learn to live without so many luxuries." Jeb, more aware of the sudden quiet than his wife, shushed her with words the storm rose up to cover.

15

Lifting her gaze, Penny took a furtive scan of the room. Everyone was dressed in black. The parlor looked like a room full of rainclouds. It had begun to feel that way, too. Did they all think like Celia, she wondered.

Just because she liked nice things, because she hadn't taken a husband and made a home for herself, well, that didn't mean she couldn't. It didn't mean she was unable to manage the running of the household and her life without her father handling every little problem.

Her mind flashed on her father, sitting at his desk in the study one room over, signing papers after carefully reading every word. Maybe Celia wasn't so very wrong. The dismal truth grayed as her new reality flashed behind her eyes, vivid as the sparks of lightning outside. What were all those papers? She hadn't a clue what kind of household business was contained in the pages that sat there right now, or what she was to do about it.

Penny suddenly realized she didn't even know how much money they had. She knew her papa had savings and investments. What were they? What should she do with them now? How would she even learn about such things now that he was gone?

Coleen O'Conner, the Irish widow who ran a boarding house, sat down beside her and interrupted the growing jumble in her mind. Coleen, a woman well into her forties had a full face that seemed a necessity so she could express all the kindness she held within her stout body. The tan she got from working her vegetable garden all spring, summer, and fall never faded much during the winter. She was a robust, healthy woman who had smiles aplenty and was never too busy to share them. Her husband had been gone for nearly ten years now, dying suddenly when his heart gave out. That was when she started renting rooms to make ends meet.

Coleen took Penny's chilly hands in her warm, plump ones. "I know, along with the grief comes the worry. I can see it on your face. Things seem bleak now. Believe me, I understand. After my Benjamin died, I had to learn a whole new life. I didn't think I could. For a while there, I just didn't know what would become of me. I suppose you're feeling a bit of that now, aren't you, girl."

Penny nodded, liking, as she always did, Coleen's foreign accent. The lilt of her speech made everything she said sound magical. It did surprise her, though, hearing such a confession. Coleen was a paragon of strength and perseverance. As far as Penny could remember, she always had been.

"We women are stronger than we're led to believe," Coleen said with a firm nod of her head, making her graying red curls bounce. "That includes you, Penny dear."

Coleen squeezed Penny's hands and gave them a little pump. "My Aunt Claire used to say a woman is like a fine bag of tea. Put us in hot water, and you'll see just how strong we really are."

Penny smiled at that; shocked she was able to do so, and hopeful, too.

"I'm going to go help Pearl in the kitchen. We'd better start putting some of that food out for people to eat," Coleen said, before giving Penny a mighty hug. Then she spoke into Penny's ear. "You'll do fine, love, now that it's required of you. You'll see." Then she leaned back a little and took Penny's wan face in her hands. "You come by and visit with me when you're feeling up to it. I'll make a pot of tea, and we'll have us a good long talk."

Before Penny could give an answer, Coleen was already making her way through the crowd toward the back of the house. At the thought of an afternoon with Coleen, a pinprick of light shone through her gloom. Yes, she would indeed go for a visit, and soon. They had much to discuss.

The front door opened on a rain-spattered gust, drawing Penny's attention. Bentley, the man who had been beside her when her father was murdered, hurried in from the storm. With him was his mother, Wilhelmina. She was a tall, broad woman, at least a head above her son, which always made him look like a child when they walked next to each other. Wilhelmina patted her coffee-colored hair, wrapped up into a bun so severe it caused her eyes to slant. Pearl took their coats and umbrellas. Bentley found Penny in short order and sat down beside her, a tad too close, with his thigh resting against hers.

"Penelope, how are you faring?"

"I…I'm doing better, Bentley. Thank you." She leaned back a little. The pomade slicking down his mousy-brown hair caused her empty stomach to roil.

"Penny…" Bentley started. Pain drew in his face and he dipped his head.

"It's all right, Bentley. No words are necessary."

He covered Penny's small hand with his. The chill of the storm crawled like an icy current from Bentley's skin, nipping a shiver all the way up her arm. He squeezed a little too hard, and his bones made an indentation in the back of her hand. Penny looked into his small eyes, close-set to a pinky-thin nose, as if to match his face, though the golden hazel color softened the harshness of his features. He pressed his lips together until they were a mere slash above the shallow quiver of his jaw. Her heart ached for Bentley. He was hurting, too.

Bentley had shown an interest in Penny, even escorted her to a dance once. She didn't share in his attraction. He was a soft-spoken man of twenty-six with a good future in banking, but Penny always sensed an inner sharpness to him, as if the creases in the neat press of his clothing were a form-fitted cosmetic to his character.

Her father thought Bentley was a nice young man, and she was just making yet another excuse to avoid a second date. Her papa had probably been right. After all, she did conjure reasons for every other suitor who'd come to call. And Bentley was ever the gentleman. Still, an attraction to him simply wasn't there.

"But, Penelope…" Bentley started again.

This time his mother cut off his words. Wilhelmina stood before them so tall she looked to be standing on a crate, which gave the illusion of her looking down her nose at Penny. Or maybe it wasn't an illusion. Wilhelmina had always been polite to her, but never kind. It was as if she worried over her son's attraction because she thought Penny unworthy. Though, considering the rein she held over her son, she probably wouldn't approve of any woman.

Wilhelmina tipped her head toward Bentley and spoke loud enough for the others to hear her over the storm. She was, in reality, making a speech to the crowd of mourners.

"Bentley, my brave, brave boy. When I think of what might have happened to you! You're so very heroic."

Bentley colored before replying in a lower voice, "Now, mother, I only did what anyone in my position would have done."

"You could have been murdered!" Bentley's mother trilled, and then shifted a quarter turn toward the quieting assembly while lifting her reticule as if to offer proof of her next statement. "I've taken to carrying smelling salts!" She then turned toward Penny and looked down without tipping her head. "Penelope, I hope you appreciate how fortunate you are. My Bentley laid down his life for you!"

Bentley looked ready to crawl under the sofa and in that moment, Penny felt sympathy for him. He'd lost his father to a riding accident almost two years ago, not long after he began working at the bank. Since then, his mother made him her entire world. Or, rather, she had taken over his world. Penny suspected his mother was the reason he gave up courting her. Not that she minded, since she didn't share feelings with Bentley, but she was sorry for him just the same.

"I hope," Wilhelmina continued. "You properly thanked my son for risking his life in order to protect you."

Had she thanked Bentley? She couldn't remember. Likely not, though. Turning to him now, Penny said, "Your mother is right, Bentley. You put yourself between that killer and me. It was a very brave and gallant thing for you to do. Thank you."

Bentley sat up straighter, clearly bolstered by her praise. "I would give my life to protect you. I only wish

I could have protected your father."

"Oh, Bentley, there was nothing you could have done. I was there. I know."

Bentley's head dropped a bit as he sighed, nodding slightly. He then looked back to her. "You're still wearing that damp dress. You really should go and change before you catch a chill."

"I'm near enough to the fire, so it's beginning to dry."

Bentley appeared concerned, but he let it go. Having nothing more to say to each other, they just sat, wedged in a silence that offered no easy exit. Pearl called everyone into the dining room where she and Coleen had laid out all of the dishes. A line formed at the end of the table, and in minutes the mourners were sitting wherever they could, though most had to stand, eating from filled plates.

At Penny's insistence, Bentley left her to get a plate for himself. She politely declined his offer to return with one for her. Pearl handed her a plate, though, urging her to eat. Penny choked down a couple bites of jam-covered bread, but mostly she shuffled the food around with her fork so it would look like she'd eaten.

As people drifted out, Penny stood by the door and thanked them for coming. Everyone was kind, offering help if she needed it, promising to stop by and check on her. Coleen folded her into her mighty arms again and repeated her invitation for tea. Penny promised she would be by soon, and she meant it. She was interested in hearing some more of Aunt Claire's wisdom.

The storm had dwindled to a light rain, but the air was damp and infused with a portentous chill. All

Penny wanted to do was to slip out of her soiled mourning clothes, crawl into her bed, and burrow beneath every blanket she could gather. She closed the door, partially glad they were gone so she could grieve in private, and yet she dreaded turning around to face an empty house. Not completely empty, she realized with a small degree of comfort, cocking an ear toward the kitchen. The wonderfully mundane sounds of Pearl washing the dishes drifted back. Once finished, though, Pearl would go to her own home, and then Penny would truly be alone.

Her hand slipped from the door. Penny hoped to be asleep by then.

"Penny."

His voice startled her, and she spun around in a rustle of black crape to see Bentley standing only a few feet away.

"Bentley. I thought you and your mother had gone."

He gestured toward the parlor, and Penny took a few steps to peer into the room. Wilhelmina slouched in a tall-backed chair, head tipped to the side, slack mouth drawing in deep breaths.

"Is she all right?" Penny asked.

"Oh yes, just napping. I'll wake her in a few minutes. I'd hoped to speak to you alone first."

"Oh, Bentley, I'm very tired. Couldn't it wait?"

"It could," he said with a businesslike tug on his vest. "But I think it best to settle a thing or two right away."

Penny nodded and allowed Bentley to lead her back into the parlor and seat her on the same sofa where she spent most of the afternoon.

"I want you to know I'm not going to abandon you, Penelope. I'm here to take care of you. There are details aplenty, and I promise I'll tend to all of them. Your father made arrangements for you in the event of his passing." He paused a moment.

The statement surprised Penny, but she said nothing.

He continued. "I thought you should know about it all as soon as possible, so you'd know you'd be cared for. I have all of the details right here." He dipped his hand into the inner pocket of his jacket and removed an envelope. From that, he slid out a thin sheaf of neatly folded papers.

"I appreciate all of your help, Bentley, truly I do. But I just can't think about business right now. I'll come down to the bank tomorrow, and you can explain it all to me then. I promise." When he looked about to persist she said, "Please, I'd really like to go and lie down now."

Frustration skittered across his face, here and gone so fast Penny couldn't swear it had been there at all.

Bentley nodded. "Of course. I understand." He tucked the papers back into his pocket. "I'll just collect mother, and we'll be off."

Waking his mother took several minutes and one good snort before her eyes popped open. Instead of being embarrassed, Wilhelmina appeared indignant at having been caught sleeping. With hasty goodbyes, they were gone.

Pearl walked in from the kitchen then, and sympathy washed over Penny. And it was overdue. It seemed she *had* been thinking only of herself. Heavy half-circles beneath Pearl's red eyes marred her pale skin. Her shoulders were drooped. It even appeared to Penny since just yesterday she'd lost weight. So caught up in her misery, it hadn't occurred to her until just then that Pearl had lost a dear, long-time friend.

"I could stay the night, if you like," Pearl said. "Or you could come back to my house and be with us. Kenny would love to have you stay for a while."

Pearl's two boys were grown up and off on their own. She lived with her husband Kenny in a modest house only a short distance away. The offer was kind and generous, as was Pearl, but Penny didn't want to keep Pearl from her home, and she didn't want to wake up tomorrow in a strange bed.

"Thank you, Pearl. That's very kind of you, but I want to stay here. I'll be fine by myself. It's best I start getting used to such things right away, don't you think?"

Pearl looked uncertain. Then making her decision, she turned toward the stairs and said, "I'm going to stay here tonight. I'll just go make sure your room is warm enough. And then…"

With two swift steps, Penny moved to take the woman by the hand. Her skin was still damp from working in the kitchen. "No. I mean it, Pearl. I have to start doing for myself. I want to. You were right all along, and not just because of the bits of conversation I heard tonight."

Pearl winced in a pained expression. "I was hoping those things got by you. This big, old house carries sound where it's not supposed to go."

"Maybe that's a good thing."

"Most of those people, Penny, well, they care about you and they're just concerned."

"I know," Penny said, believing her. Only a couple of the comments she'd heard had ill intent. Most did sound as though they were purely worried about her. "I have a lot of thinking to do," she told Pearl. "You go home now. Be with your husband. I'll be fine, truly I will."

After a moment, the older woman gave a reluctant nod and turned to the rack by the door to retrieve her coat.

"And Pearl."

Pearl twisted around as she slid her arms into her sleeves.

"Papa always knew how lucky we've been to have you in our lives."

Pearl fastened her coat as if giving thought to each button, a noticeable tremble in her hands. When she raised her head, Pearl's gathering tears seeped into Penny's heart. Penny flew into the arms of the woman who'd looked after her since she was a little girl, and they held on, each trying to ease the other's grief. After a moment, Pearl took her by the shoulders and leaned back.

"Your father pampered you, but you're not spoiled rotten. You're a good girl and smart, too. Don't let anyone tell you different."

Penny smiled a little, wiping at her own tears. "Thank you."

"Oh," Pearl said, pivoting. "Look at me. I forgot to put out the lamps in the parlor. Are you done in there?"

"Yes, but I'll get them," Penny said, smiling at Pearl's wide-eyed reaction. "I'm going to start doing things for myself. I mean it. Lots of things, like cooking. I want to learn how to cook."

Pearl's eyebrows shot up.

"You've been at me for a long time to learn, and well, as I said, you were right. It's one of many things I should know."

Pearl nodded and even smiled a little, looking as proud as she would of her own children. "All right. We'll start this week. Tomorrow, if you like."

"Tomorrow is your day off, Pearl."

"Well, normally, but I thought I should—"

"You stay home with Kenny tomorrow and tend to your own business. In fact, take the next day, too. You've worked long and hard today. All of this has been difficult, and you haven't even had proper time to grieve."

Pearl shook her head. "Oh, Penny, I don't think…"

"I insist. No arguments," Penny said with more strength than she felt. She was trying to feel it, thinking about Coleen's Aunt Claire and wanting to be as strong as a good bag of tea. Just recalling those words helped.

"But you'll be here all alone."

"I have a lot of thinking to do. I *need* to be alone for a little while."

After a moment, Pearl said, "Well, only if you promise to come get me if you need me, for anything at all."

"I promise." From where she stood, Penny could see out the parlor window, tapped now with only light droplets. The winds had dwindled to a breeze, but the sun hung low on the horizon, and it was getting colder by the minute.

"It's almost dark, Pearl. Go home while you can still see out there. I'm just going to bed now anyway."

After another hug and a reluctant goodbye, Pearl

left. Penny closed the door and wandered back into the parlor. She lingered there for no particular reason. Exhaustion dragged on her and she needed to go to bed, but her mind was suddenly abuzz, so she rambled about the room where she and her father had spent so much time together.

Faint echoes of what she'd heard earlier haunted her thoughts, goaded her with the worst possible scenarios. Shifting her gaze upward, she could see, as if there were no barrier, her grand collection of dresses and shoes, of bonnets, petticoats, ribbons, ruffles, and so much finery that took up most of the spare bedroom. What she owned all for herself could likely clothe many women for a good long time. She thought now of the women she knew. Some had dresses they'd worn for years, with faded colors and oft-mended hems. Of course, they thought her spoiled. How could they not when she paraded by them regularly with something new?

Shame nipped at her heels, so Penny walked some more. Maybe she could shake it before it followed her upstairs.

She let her hand drag across the top of the shiny piano where many a night she'd played and sang for her father. Pausing at the small table beside the Melas rug, she let her fingers rest gently upon the Swiss Rosewood music box he had given her for her sixteenth birthday. Butterflies adorned the wood, painted in yellow and gold with a few splashes of red. She could hum every note of the enchanting ballad, having listened to it so very many times. Today, the lid stayed closed beneath the reverent touch of her fingertips. She wasn't that strong yet.

The fire had dwindled to nothing, and the room was cooling fast. Though she hadn't gone upstairs yet, Penny already knew Pearl had lit the fire in her room, and it would be warm when she walked through the door. That was something else she should start doing for herself. Keeping her mind pointed in that direction seemed a constructive way to avoid the hungry sorrow threatening to swallow her whole.

Rubbing her arms with her hands, Penny walked to the window. Strands of deepening purple wove through the charcoal gray sky. They dissipated before touching ground. Soon there would be no light at all. Still, she stood there staring blankly at the world in which she now lived alone. She shivered once, and then wrapped her arms around herself before taking and releasing a deep, shaky breath. Turning from the window, Penny walked through the room using the brass knobs to twist down the mantles on each kerosene lamp before blowing out the flames. *It's a start.*

In her bedroom, a fire blazed behind the grate. The room was warm and her bed turned down. She would start doing these things for herself, but tonight she was grateful Pearl had done them for her. She changed from her heavy dress to her nightgown and burrowed into the covers, but she didn't fall asleep for a good many hours.

Penny spent most of the night rearranging the contents of her head.

Chapter 4

After leaving his horse at the livery, Garrett took his time walking through town. The morning was bright with only a few wisps of white clouds floating on the horizon and sunshine making a decent effort to nudge out the chill. The streets were still muddy and pockmarked with puddles of various sizes, but the storm had moved on, thank the powers that be. He thanked them again, because he'd found shelter last night with a benevolent farm family before the worst of it hit.

Mill's Creek was as he remembered, small but civilized and well tended, with swept boardwalks along the storefronts. The windows all looked wiped of dust and smudges. Shop owners maintained the simple wood plank buildings, right down to the steps in front of their businesses. The water in the public horse troughs was fresh and free of scum. The town wasn't fancy, but it was clean and cared for.

Two young women, one with light brown hair and one with a head of red, both dressed in simple calico walked toward him. Their gazes latched onto him about ten seconds after he noticed them. The redhead was the first to lock eyes on him, slowing her step and ceasing conversation. Her friend followed her line of sight and did the same.

"Ladies," Garrett said, tipping his hat.

They both giggled before answering in unison, "Marshal."

The one with red hair let her admiring stare linger until her blushing friend tugged her arm and dragged her past him. They left a trail of giggles and whispers in their wake, though he couldn't make out what they were saying. Eventually, their sounds faded away.

Half a block later, Garrett paused as if someone had called his name, and his head tipped back for a sniff. Though he couldn't tell which direction it was coming from, he caught the unmistakable aroma of baking bread. The air suddenly seemed full with it, warmer, too. It brought to mind delicious memories of home cooking, and that made him think about his family.

Work kept him busy. He hadn't seen his mother or his younger brother and sister in almost four months, the longest stretch yet. Garrett closed his eyes and drew in the warm smell of bread again. The aroma connected his mind to family meals, to the good-natured teasing, to all he'd gone without during his relentless pursuit of every outlaw that needed catching.

It didn't matter that even if he worked twenty-four hours a day, he couldn't get all of them. He still meant to try. Meanwhile, the years were passing quickly. *Too quickly*. A future filled with criminals and endless days on their trails loomed. Here he was, twenty-eight years old and he'd yet to start a family of his own.

Lately, on his endless travels, on the long nights sleeping on hard ground alone, or with some worthless outlaw tied to a nearby tree, he'd begun to think about how good it would be to settle down with a nice, simple woman. Not yet, though.

Garrett couldn't even consider such a life at this time, not when there was so much that needed doing. Predators were on the loose, innocent people were dying; there was too much lawlessness in this world for him to think of a wife and children. He didn't have time, and no woman should have to settle for the scraps he could offer. When he settled this matter, he decided with another good whiff of baking bread, he'd go home for a visit and get himself reacquainted with his own family. Before he could think about even that taste of personal comfort, he had a killer to catch.

The townspeople he passed were quick with a smile and a tip of their heads in a pleasant hello. It was a friendly town; yet with the exception of the two young ladies, the cheer in the greetings he received was subdued. He could feel it. He could see it in their caution. It was fresh and ill fit. There'd been a murder here, one of their own. Life would go on, but it would not be the same.

The outskirts of the town spread wide over many miles. The heart of Mill's Creek, the part where some people lived and others rode in to do their business, was small. Only two blocks one way and two the other, not a lot of frills. One hotel with a restaurant, a mercantile, albeit a sizable one, a livery, a telegraph office, and a ranch supply store along with a few other little shops and businesses. The town did host three saloons, he noted with a half-smile. At least two of them had rooms upstairs where he was sure many a ranch hand spent his pay.

Several ranches and farms subsisted within just a few miles. None of them, however, was huge. This town didn't host enough wealth to gain the attention of a bank robber.

Usually someone willing to kill a man and risk the gallows to rob a bank would set his sights on a larger town where he could get a much bigger take for his trouble. There were several within only a two- or three-day ride. Why would the outlaw pick this town?

A few answers to his question sprung to mind; desperation, drunkenness, lack of forethought. It could also be since it is such a small town; the outlaw believed he could be in and out without any trouble. Maybe the banker had tried to stop him and things just turned bad.

As Garrett approached the mercantile, he came upon a man sweeping the boards in front of the store. He was a thin man in a clean white apron with a few brown hairs combed neatly over the crown of his narrow head. At the sound of Garrett's boots, he looked up to nod a friendly greeting. Then for just a flash, the man looked surprised, even a bit wary. Garrett was used to that. As a man who stood six foot three with a broad build, well, sometimes people got the feeling simply by virtue of his size he could be dangerous. And of course, the town had just suffered a terrible crime. Then the man's gaze caught on the silver star pinned to Garrett's shirt pocket, visible since his duster hung open.

"Mornin', Marshal," the man said with a grin that bespoke relief.

"Morning."

"Jeb Carter," the man said, stilling his broom and holding it in front of him as he straightened his back. "You here to catch the bastard that killed Frank Wills?"

"Name's Kinkaid, and yes, I am. You see anything that day?"

"No. Came runnin' out when I heard the shots. We don't get much of that kind of stuff around here, and never had nothin' like this. Usually it's just some drunken fool wandering out of a saloon thinkin' to shoot at the moon. This was right in the middle of the day. He rode out the other end of town. All I saw was dust. Surely do wish I could help. Frank was a good man. Not one of those stuffed shirt types you find in the big cities, the guys who do their jobs with all head and no heart. You know the type I'm talkin' about?"

"I do."

"It's a cryin' shame, that's what it is. I don't know what's going to happen to poor little Penny."

"Who's Penny?"

"Penny Wills, Frank's daughter."

So the man had a family. The murder was striking close to home, and that didn't bode well for the killer once Garrett got his hands on him. Oh, he'd bring him back to stand trial, all right. He didn't hold with vigilante justice. With the slightest provocation, however, he'd turn over the killer, as John Gladwin had put it, 'a mite damaged.'

"What about the girl's mother?" Garrett asked.

"Oh, Mary died when Penny was six or seven. She ain't got nobody else."

A child left without any family because of one man's greed and lack of respect for human life. Garrett's gut tightened in conjunction with his fists. The image strove to leave him feeling weak and helpless. But he was neither. He had a badge, a gun, and he was well versed in both. While he couldn't bring the little girl's father back, he could make damn sure she got justice, and he'd see to it the killer never did this to

33

anyone else.

"Jeb!" a woman's harsh voice called from inside the store. "You got Sam at the back door."

"Coming," Jeb shouted back.

"Nice to meet you, Marshal. I surely do hope you catch that snake-belly."

"I will," answered Garrett, confident he would. That wasn't arrogance talking, either. The plain fact was Garrett had brought to trial every outlaw he'd ever sought. Except, that is, for the few who foolishly thought they could outgun him. Those men bypassed the trial and drove themselves straight to execution.

Jeb carried his broom into the store, muttering under his breath about a snake-bellied bastard. Garrett headed for the sheriff's office.

When he stepped inside, he found the portly sheriff tipped back in his chair with his feet propped up on the desk, snoring loud enough to loosen the bricks. He had a pillow tucked behind his head of bushy brown hair and another one under his bootless feet. Garrett shut the door behind him, hard. The sheriff jumped, nearly rolling from his beleaguered chair. Awkwardly, he managed to get to his feet, thick brows drawn in annoyance at the intrusion, until he caught sight of the badge pinned to Garrett's chest.

"Marshal." He coughed to clear the sleep from his throat before saying, "Hello. I'm Sheriff McElroy."

"Garrett Kincaid," he stated to the soft man who didn't look like he could subdue his baby sister in a fight, unless he fell on her.

He guessed the sheriff to be about thirty-five years old. He stood five foot seven or so, with a ruddy complexion and weighed enough for two sheriffs. He had a soft look about him, like bread dough that had risen and was ready to bake. The bulge around his middle stressed his buttons. The way Garrett had just walked right in without him even knowing it, having had to slam the door just to get him to wake up, didn't speak well of the man's instincts.

"Oh, um, Marshal. Come in, come in. Glad you're here. I…um, I don't usually sleep in the middle of the day like this," the sheriff said, looking embarrassed as he glanced at his pillows, caught in an obvious lie. His eyes darted a moment before meeting Garrett's. "It's just that, well, I've been working myself to the bone since the robbery and murder."

"You've worked yourself to the bone in two days?" Garrett asked. Before the man could respond with any more nonsense Garrett said, "What information have you gotten from the witnesses?"

"Well, the people who were in the bank are too upset to talk to right now. I figured I'd give them some time, let their minds rest a little before questioning them."

Astonished, Garrett said, "You haven't spoken to them yet, not at all?" Once again, he put forth a second question before the sheriff could answer the first. "What about the people who were outside the bank?"

After a moment of sputtering, Sheriff McElroy said, "I don't think anybody saw anything."

"You don't *think*?"

"Well, I haven't talked to anybody yet."

"Because you've been out riding with a posse of men, men properly suited to the job, instructed, and sworn in?" Garrett asked, sarcasm flagging his suspicion because he was sure that wasn't the case. He was equally sure the sheriff was in over his head with this. Likely, his job had never entailed anything more taxing than throwing a drunk into his single cell for a night. Still, McElroy had sworn himself to a duty here, and if he couldn't do the work, he should find another job.

"A posse?" the sheriff questioned, his thumbs slipping into his taut suspenders, hands sliding up and down while his mind stirred up some indignation. "Now see here, I don't care for your attitude. The fact is I had to stay put. I'm the only law here. Someone had to be here to protect the good people of this town."

"Lucky people," Garrett muttered under his breath as he turned toward the door. It was just as well the sheriff hadn't gathered any of the local folk. A town like this was hardly fraught with posse material. More likely than not one of them would get killed. No, it was best if he handled this alone.

"Where are you going?" McElroy asked.

"To work," Garrett replied before closing the door behind him.

Aside from the jail, the bank was the only brick building in town. There was a large window in the front wall and a smaller pane of glass in the door where a "Closed" sign presently hung. Garrett turned the knob and stepped inside.

The place was small, a short counter with room for one clerk and an orderly desk off to the side. The low, wooden wall closing off the back would be a simple thing to step over, though Garrett didn't think even that much effort had been necessary. A gate in the wall was propped open. Even if closed it wouldn't have mattered, as there was no lock, just a latch. In the back wall was

36

the safe. Not very large, but then, it was probably as big as was needed. The door to the safe was opened part way.

Again, Garrett considered the size of the bank. He could understand why someone wouldn't go to a big city to commit his crime, more obstacles, more danger, and the chance of getting caught was much greater. But there were plenty of small towns larger than this that would have been a much better get with only slightly more risk. The reasons he'd considered earlier returned to his mind, along with a new one. If the robber had any knowledge at all as to what kind of sheriff this town had, he knew getting away would be easy.

A young clerk with a head of curly blond hair rebelling against his pomade stood behind the counter reviewing a ledger and making notes on a separate piece of paper. He raised his head when Garrett walked in, sliding a pair of round spectacles up his nose. Garrett gave him an acknowledging nod. The clerk quietly returned it.

At a scraping sound, Garrett turned toward a man who was kneeling on the floor, a tin bucket at his side. The man had a large brush in his hands. He was using it to scrub a bloodstain from the boards. Beside him stood a man somewhere near to Garrett's age. He was dressed in a soft gray sack coat with matching waistcoat and trousers. His shoes were shiny. In his hands, he held a bowler hat of the same color.

Turning from the stain at his feet, the man looked at Garrett and said in a clipped voice, "We're not open today."

"You're open for me," Garrett said, lifting aside his duster to show his badge while stalking toward the man who appeared to be in charge.

"Oh, Marshal," he said, taking a step toward Garrett before turning back to the man on the floor. "If you can't scrub it out then replace the boards.

"Name's Kincaid," Garrett said as soon as the man faced him again.

"Hello. I'm Bentley Werner. I'm…I'm in charge here now."

"Were you in here during the robbery?"

"Yes. I worked for Frank Wills." He paused, confusion creasing his face. "I'm not sure why you're here. We have a sheriff, and I'm confident he is perfectly capable of handling the situation."

"Your confidence is misplaced." The man looked insulted. Town pride, Garrett figured. Before the man could argue he said, "Bank robbery is a federal crime. The murder was committed during the robbery."

"I see. Well, things happened very fast, and he had a bandana covering his face, so I don't think I can offer you much help."

"How many robbers were there?"

"Just the one."

"What did he look like?"

"I…I couldn't really say. As I already told you, his face was covered."

"What color hair did he have?"

"Oh, um, well, I believe it was brown."

"What color were his eyes?"

"Hmm. I don't know."

"Was he a tall man, heavy, thin?"

Bentley huffed out a breath and rubbed his ear in an agitated fashion. "As I said, everything happened quickly. I just didn't notice those things. All I remember is that gun, and what he did with it."

"Who else was in here when the robbery took place?"

"Neil over there," he said, motioning toward the clerk behind the counter. "He can't help you, though. He fainted as soon as he saw the gun."

Garrett turned toward the clerk. "Can you tell me what you saw, heard, anything at all about the robber?"

"Sorry, sir. Mr. Werner is right," the clerk said, looking as if he wanted to crawl into a hole. "I was unconscious during most of the robbery."

Turning back to Bentley, Garrett asked, "Was anybody else in here at the time?"

"Just us."

"No customers?"

"We're a small town, Marshal, and it was a slow period. Happens a lot."

Neil spoke up then. "Miss Penny was here."

Bentley issued a sour expression to the clerk, who flushed deeper and proceeded to dive back into his ledger.

"Penny Wills?" Garrett asked, shooting a sharp look on Bentley. "Frank Wills' daughter? You forgot to mention her, Mr. Werner."

"This has been a terrible ordeal for her, as you can imagine. She witnessed her father's murder. Besides, she was standing behind me most of the time and saw less than I did, so, she really can't help you. You'll just have to make do without her. I don't want her further upset."

"I'll take all that into consideration when I talk to her."

"Now see here…"

Before Bentley could finish his sentence, the door to the bank flew open. Garrett turned to see a young woman enter; a vision, really, flushed, breathless, as if she'd been running. Her determined eyes alight with ire. Though she was wearing a dress of prim black layers from foot to throat, letting him only guess at her form, she had a face the finest artists striving for perfection could not have accurately formed.

Even the heaviness beneath her wide eyes marking her sleeplessness could not mar their emerald color, tinted with flecks of gold that held a glow even from across the room. She wore her hair, the hue of freshly washed lemons, all of it tucked into a small black bonnet, leaving him to wonder at the length. Her alabaster skin bore not a single flaw, so soft in appearance it made a man's hand ache to touch it. Her nose had a tiny upturn with nary a freckle. Full lips with a pink tinge that in the space of a few accelerated beats of his heart stole every thought he had but the carnal ones.

For a moment, she locked eyes with Garrett. And for just that instant, the rest of his world paled to gone, like night to the morn. All he could see was this woman. Again, it struck him how her face appeared too perfect to be real, the rendering of an artistic angel. Garrett blinked, hard, disoriented even, thinking he couldn't possibly be seeing her clearly. He was, though. For when he focused on her again, he held no doubt she was indeed a flesh and blood woman, albeit the most exquisite creature he'd ever seen. The young woman spun, then, directing her hostility toward Bentley.

"You should have told me the marshal was here. If I hadn't gone into the mercantile I wouldn't have even known."

"Penelope, you should be home resting. I'll handle this."

Penelope. This was Penny, Garrett realized, the murdered man's daughter. She wasn't a child, though, but a grown woman, young, but grown. That explained the weight of her eyes. It also explained her eagerness to see the lawman who had come to town to catch her father's killer.

Poor little Penny, the man at the mercantile had said. Looking at her now, no one would think her wilting under the stress of what she'd witnessed. Her spine was as straight as a fine aim, her shoulders pulled back, imparting dignity and fortitude to her carriage. She looked ready to challenge the world, not hide from it. After what she'd gone through, he had to give her due respect.

Whipping his wits into shape, Garrett said, "You're Frank Wills' daughter?" She turned to him, so clean and fresh she was a million miles from anything he'd seen in months.

"Yes, Marshal," said Bentley. "This is Miss Penelope Wills. Penelope, Marshal Kincaid."

"My condolences," Garrett said, removing his hat and placing it on the edge of the desk without really looking.

"Thank you. Have you…"

A couple entered the bank then, and everyone turned toward the door. The man was dressed in well-worn work trousers and a shirt to match. The woman, however, wore a sunny yellow gown with a matching bonnet and looked properly fit to attend a ball.

"Are you open for business yet?" the man asked

Bentley.

"Tomorrow, Burt. We'll be open tomorrow." Then, to no one in particular, Bentley said, "Doesn't anybody read a sign anymore?"

After they left, Bentley stared a moment as they passed by the front window before turning a baffled expression to Penny. "Penelope, was Lucy wearing one of your dresses?"

"Yes. I gave it to her this morning."

Something outside the window caught Bentley's attention, and he scrunched up his face as he moved closer to the glass. His head swiveled one way and then swung sharply the other. At the same time, his hands shot to the windowsill. His nose rubbed against the glass as he strained to peer down the street. "Penny, several of the townswomen are wearing your dresses."

Garrett took a good look out the window. A woman passed by, and two more across the street wearing dresses of varying styles and colors, all lovely, all looking brand new.

"I spent the morning giving away most of my dresses and skirts and blouses," Penny told Bentley.

"Giving them away!" He swung around from the window and marched a few steps toward her.

"Yes. Bonnets, too." She turned to Garrett then. "Marshal, have you caught the man who murdered my father?"

"Penelope, why would you give away all of your clothing?" an irate Bentley asked.

Barely sparing him a glance, she said, "I didn't give everything away. I kept what I need. Marshal?"

Back to business, Garrett said, "No. I haven't arrested anyone yet. I will, though. Can you tell me anything about the man who shot your father? I understand his face was covered, but did you notice anything about him, size, his clothing, maybe the color of his eyes?"

"I got a good look at his face," she said, stunning the marshal.

Garrett shot an accusatory scowl toward Bentley. "You told me his face was covered."

"It was," said Bentley, defensive and cowering a bit under the marshal's glare. "He came in with a red bandana tied over his face."

"Yes," Penny cut in. "It was covered when he came in, but he must not have tied it tight enough because it fell off."

"It fell off, did it?" he said, directing his words toward Bentley before shifting his eyes back to Penny.

Bentley said, "Well, that was right at the end, and it was only for a moment. Not enough time to really see him."

Ignoring him completely now, Garrett said to Penny, "Tell me everything you can remember about him, Miss Wills."

Penny looked directly at Garrett and said, "He was filthy. I can tell you that. He smelled as though he hadn't bathed in a year. He was taller than Bentley here, but at least three or four inches shorter than you, Marshal. He had a bit of a belly, but he looked strong. His hair was probably blond, but it was very dirty and so it's hard to say for sure and impossible to tell the shade. He had dark brown eyes, and his beard was two or three inches long. It was uneven, mangled, and dirty, and he had a terrible scar on his face that cut into his beard. It was a raised scar, and light pink and hair didn't grow on it. It was right here." She ran an index finger along her face showing the marshal exactly where and how long the scar had been.

"His teeth were brown and rotting," Penny continued. "His clothes and boots were old and caked with dirt. He carried a knife at his waist, a rather large one. It was oddly clean with a nickel inlay. Oh, and his voice was rough and gravely, if that's any help." She thought for a moment. "I think that's everything. I wish I could tell you more."

Garrett had seen lawmen less able to give such a detailed description. Brains wrapped in a pretty package. The wholeness of her stifled his voice for a moment or two. Finally, Garrett cleared his throat and said, "You did well, Miss Wills. Very well."

"Please call me Penny."

"Penny. You've a sharp mind. That's far more information than I've gotten from the other two witnesses combined." Garrett couldn't help but throw that in, slanting a sharp glance toward Bentley. However, the man didn't notice him at all. He was gawking at Penny as though she was a creature from another world.

Penny simply nodded. Her ego seemed untouched by his praise. A small frown line appeared between her elegant brows as she thought harder, trying to remember anything else that might be of some help. That's what he figured, anyway. Or maybe she was grappling with the terrible memory of what she'd witnessed here in this very room a mere two days ago.

"That scar," Garret said, his memory speaking aloud while his eyes stayed on Penny, stuck like a fly in molasses. A part of him knew his voice was speaking independent of his brain; however, the knowledge was too disengaged to keep the words behind his teeth. "A couple years back I arrested a man fitting such a description, had a scar just like that. He was part of a group of cattle rustlers. He was particularly fond of knives. If I remember right, name was Zeke Cotter."

"Zeke Cotter," Penny said, thinking on the name and then saying it again. "I can't say I've ever heard of him. Either of you?"

Bentley and the clerk both shook their heads.

Garrett immediately yanked his gaze away from Penny to stare out the front window while he mentally gave himself a good sock in the jaw. Another one of those fancy dresses floated by, something pink with white lace. He barely noticed. He couldn't believe he'd just said that name out loud. He knew better than that. These people were grieved and angry. The last thing he should be doing is giving them a name to chase. Talk about asking for trouble. What had happened to his good sense?

The answer was standing there right in front of him, beguiling as a lily in moonlight, and though it was mulish, he could not accept a pretty face had set him so off kilter. His problem was he'd been too long at the job without a break, and way too long without the sweet comforts of a woman.

After vowing to remedy both of those situations in the near future, Garrett turned to Bentley and said, "Can you at least tell me how much money was taken?"

Bentley gave his waistcoat a dignified tug and said, "Of course I can tell you. It was almost six hundred dollars. Neil can give you the exact amount."

"That's all?" Garrett and Penny said at the same

time.

Penny marched through the open gate to the back wall of the bank where she peered inside the safe that was open about a third of the way. She then twisted back toward Garrett, surprise evident on her face. "He didn't take any of the money from in here."

Garrett walked to the back and stood beside Penny. He caught a whiff of rosewater. It smelled even better than the bread, stirring appetites he'd just vowed to appease. A reminder the girl had just lost her father and that his thoughts were turning wholly inappropriate helped shame him back to work. It still took a force of will before he could focus on the inside of the safe.

It was tidy, not the sloppy scattering of papers shoved aside in a rush to grab the money. Nor were there any stray bills lying here or there that had escaped a hasty looting. Cash sat stacked in neat bundles, most of them wrapped and placed in perfect order on the three shelves. In the corner was a single, four tier wooden file cabinet. The drawers all shut, nice and neat. Nothing at all appeared to have been disturbed.

"Was the safe open when he was here?" Garrett asked.

"Yes, it was," answered Penny.

It was easy to understand why she sounded so baffled. Garrett was right there with her. A man risked life and limb to rob a bank, yet left the open safe untouched?

To Bentley he said, "Was anything missing from the files?"

Bentley shook his head. "He never went in there at all."

Penny tipped her head up until her eyes met

Garrett's. "But there was a pause in their footsteps, my father's and the robber's. It was when I was standing behind Bentley." She turned to Bentley, then. "I assumed he was collecting the money from the safe."

Bentley said, "No, he never even looked in there. He must have panicked and left without thinking about the safe."

"What made him panic," Garrett asked. He walked back through the gate toward the center of the room. Penny followed. "Did Mr. Wills argue with him?"

"No!" Penny nearly shouted. "My father was completely cooperative. He spoke calmly and did everything asked of him. That man had no reason to…" Her voice caught.

Tears threatened, but she managed to shore up. However, Garrett could see it was a strain on her fortitude, and he felt like a brute putting her through this.

"No reason to do what he did," Penny finished.

Garrett resisted the urge to put his arm around her. Somebody should, though. He shot quick glances toward the other two other men in the room. They knew her. Likely, they'd known her for years. It was their place to offer comfort. Neither of them did.

Bentley said, "He probably panicked when his bandana fell off. It was right after that when he shot Mr. Wills."

"The both of you saw his face, too," Garrett pointed out. "Did he aim the gun at either one of you?"

"No, he didn't," Penny said. "We saw him plain as day. Why wouldn't he kill us, too?"

She looked to Garrett who gave a small nod, as that was also his question.

"He probably intended to also kill us," Bentley said. "People don't think straight when they panic. It was a very stressful situation, Marshal."

It wasn't completely implausible. He shot the gun, could have even been by accident. Once he realized he'd killed a man, he panicked and ran before he gave thought to the other two witnesses. Still, things weren't sitting right.

Bentley continued. "After shooting Frank three times, he had to know others would hear the shots and come running."

"He shot your father three times?" Garrett asked Penny as gently as he could. It was a horrible question to put to her, but if he wanted a straight answer, he already knew she was the one to ask.

Penny answered with a nod. The muscles in her throat tightened, and her entire body appeared to sag at the memory. She grasped her hands together in front of her skirt, squeezing.

Garrett saw her fighting to hold back the tears. With a deep breath, she managed to collect her emotions and tuck them away, at least for the time being. She wouldn't have this grief under control indefinitely. At some point, she'd have to let it out. She was managing well, though, or maybe not. It was an odd thing she'd done, giving away her clothes. But it wasn't his business. Catching the killer was.

Garrett stood still as Penny straightened her shoulders and tipped her head back until her eyes once again met his. Bright emerald in color, they were like jewels of the finest cut, glittering, captivating. It's no wonder Zeke Cotter's name slipped from his lips. Looking at her was like staring into the eyes of a mythological siren, as if she'd cast a spell, and his mind was not fully under his control. Garrett had the feeling if he wasn't careful that might be a lingering condition.

"I think Bentley is right," Penny said. "Once that man pulled the trigger he certainly knew he was in danger of getting caught. Of course he ran."

Garrett nodded, turning away from her while experience and common sense told him different. Three witnesses, three bullets fired, yet all used to kill just one; leaving the other two able to not only identify him, but testify against him should he be caught.

"Did your father have any enemies?" Garrett asked.

"No, of course not," she responded, her brows drawn together. "Everybody loved him. Why, you should have been at our house after the funeral and you would have seen. As terrible as that storm was, everybody showed up just to say nice things about him."

Garrett nodded. Frank Wills could have had enemies his daughter didn't know about. A man in his line of work, where people's livelihoods could well depend on his decisions, it was entirely possible someone was angry over a financial matter. Could be he didn't want to worry his daughter by informing her of some dispute. It was also possible Mr. Wills had angered someone and didn't even realize it himself. Maybe the killer shot him over something that had nothing at all to do with the bank. That would explain the untouched safe. It wouldn't be the first time Garrett had seen a man murdered over something other than money. He'd seen people lose their lives over all kinds of things, some downright meaningless.

Done with the interview, Werner said, "Penelope, I think you should go home right now and lie down."

"I'm fine, Bentley."

"You most certainly are not. Your mind is all muddled. You're not thinking clearly. Later I want you to give me a list of the women who now have your dresses. I'll go around and collect them for you."

"You'll do no such thing, Bentley. My mind is perfectly clear. More clear than it's ever been, in fact. My life is different now. I have to approach things accordingly, and that's exactly what I'm doing. I had an excess of clothing and a deficiency of respect. Today I've simply taken steps to rectify both of those situations."

"Respect?" Bentley said, as if she'd spoken a great insult to herself. "You're one of the most respected people in this town."

"My father was. I attained my respect by way of association. Besides, I was referring to the respect I feel toward myself." At his baffled expression, Penny said, "Bentley, the fact is I've lived a life of frivolity, and I've decided on a course of action. Paring down my wardrobe was only the first step. The next thing I plan to do is…" and then her eye caught for the first time on the other man in the bank, the one who was down on his knees.

What little color she had drained from her face and Garrett followed her line of sight. The man was still kneeling on the floor scrubbing away her father's blood. The water in the bucket beside him was pink and gray, the straw-colored bristles of his scrub brush coated in red. Damn, he'd completely forgotten about that. Had he been thinking at all, he would have had the stain covered and sent the man away. He turned back to Penny to see her tip her head to the side, and then her eyes lost focus before closing completely. Garrett caught her before she hit the floor.

Chapter 5

Penny awoke to a blank slate.

She instantly recognized her surroundings. There was the wallpaper she'd chosen, yellow as a sunflower in spring adorned with white daisies. Across from the bed, her oak dressing table topped with Swiss lace upon which sat her creams and her silver brushes. Against the other wall was her oversized armoire. In the corner sat the washstand with her white, blue-vined basin and a matching jug of water. The familiarity of the room, however, did not ease the prevalence of confusion.

She was lying on her bed, fully dressed in the middle of the day. Since she never napped, she wondered how that happened. Turning her head, she glanced out her bedroom window, which faced the front of the house. The gingham curtain was open. Skeletal branches of the elm just outside provided scant breaks in the sunlight, as if the window suffered a minor spray of cracks. In a few weeks, those branches would host sprouting leaves, unfurling to act as a filter to give blessed shade during the summer to come. For now though, brightness flowed through the glass with such gusto she had to squint to look out, telling her it was early afternoon.

Then, with the speed of a sudden death, Penny remembered everything. The morning spent distributing a good portion of her wardrobe, Bentley, the marshal, and the man on the floor of the bank washing away her father's blood. She rolled toward the wall and curled up on her side as her stomach roiled at the memory.

Her poor, sweet father who never harmed a soul, murdered at the hands of an outlaw. Her fists clenched into tight little balls, eyes closed, arms squeezed to her chest as if she could crush the pain from her heart.

For several minutes, she stayed that way, battling the torrents of horror and grief, hoping someday soon she would become numb to them. When the darkness threatened to keep her, she opened her eyes and faced it. Someone had laid a blanket over her. The temptation to burrow beneath it was strong, but she fought that off, too. It seemed battles of all sorts now beset her life.

She flung the blanket aside and slowly, testing the sway of the room, sat up, and put her feet over the edge of the bed. Her shoes sat there, nice and neat, with the laces tucked inside. She slipped them on her feet and tied them before stepping out of the room. The voices coming from downstairs in the parlor made her pause at the railing. Bentley's voice she recognized right away. Then the marshal's deep timbre arose in response.

Though she well knew it was wrong to eavesdrop, Penny stayed where she was. In part because she was embarrassed at having fainted, and that she did so for the first time in her life in front of Marshal Kincaid, of all things. For some reason she cared what he thought of her. He was the last thing she should be thinking about right now. But think of him she did.

At the bank, she'd been concentrating on her questions, but she'd have to be blind not to notice he was a finely built man. His body exuded power, and not just because of his size. The marshal's shirt clung to

53

firm muscle. His movements were sure, confident. He was a man who knew his job. Of his physical attributes, what stood out to her most, however, were his eyes, blue steel that softened to a comfortable cerulean whenever they fell upon her. It was as if the course of his job had hardened him, or maybe the course of his life, perhaps both. Yet when his gaze met hers, Penny saw a tender side to the man.

The marshal was handsome, certainly, with a strong-jawed face, ruggedly tanned, impressed with faint lines demarking thought and concentration. Dark hair recently cut, yet he was clearly not persnickety because it looked finger-combed. Penny didn't know why she found such a thing endearing, but she did.

What truly drew her to the man, though, was the way he behaved toward her. Marshal Kincaid was kind, but not piteous, never once treating her as if she couldn't cross the street without a hand to hold onto. In fact, he treated her as an adult. That was a first for her, Penny realized now. She was determined it wouldn't be the last.

The marshal listened to what she had to say, too, and not with half an ear. Funny, how she hadn't recognized before that's what people often did when conversing with her. It was her own doing, she supposed. Thinking on it now it was as if she'd spent her life portraying a silly, trivial character from a poorly written play. There was a whole part of her, a better part, which she'd kept hidden away, even from her father. Why? Why would she do that?

Penny had thoughts that dove deeper than fashion and fun. She read, and not just for entertainment. She read whatever newspaper her father finished and discarded. She kept up with current events and did so with interest, not obligation. Nobody knew about that, not even her papa, not really. It seems she had played the part for him, too. Or had she simply been living up to the role in which life cast her?

If that was the case, it was time to rewrite the text. Maybe she had already. At the very least, she'd begun, and she must be off to a good start. Marshal Kincaid treated her differently than any man ever had. Or woman, for that matter, with the exception of Coleen O'Conner, bless her big, Irish heart.

The marshal took in everything Penny had to say with the same respect he allotted to Bentley. Maybe more, now that she thought about it. In fact, he'd told her she had a sharp mind, said it right in front of everyone. The accolade was earnest, too, not used as a tool of courtship, as she'd encountered in the past. A smile actually tugged on her lips as she recalled the shocked look on Bentley's face at her fine description of the robber. She *had* done well, had in fact done better than either of the two men who had been in the bank that day.

It was a new experience in her new life, being treated so. Terrible as the circumstances under which it had been unveiled, she liked having someone take her seriously. She'd discovered a whole new side to herself, and she liked it, a lot. So far, her steps in a new direction were small, but they were hers. She would take more. First, though, she would see the man who killed her father punished.

"Penelope is a fragile thing," Bentley said from the parlor.

Penny bristled as she peered at them from her place

at the banister. Bentley's shadow crossed back and forth across the sunlit room. She recognized the neat clip of his steps. The marshal's shadow was there, too, tall and solid. His arms were crossed, she could tell. Broad shoulders topped his strength, and a lift of his head implied he was just the slightest bit arrogant. He wasn't moving. He appeared the perfection of a statue, a monument of justice erected in the wilds. Good lord, even his shadow was masculine. Next to him, Bentley's shadow looked like a woodland creature patrolling the forest grounds all in a tizzy.

"I don't intend to abuse her," the marshal replied. "I just have a few more questions for her. She has the most honest and accurate recollection of all of you by far."

Penny pressed her fingers against her mouth to keep the bark of laughter from giving her away. That statement most certainly irritated Bentley. She didn't know why that gave her pleasure, but it did. She placed her hands on the smooth oak of the banister and relished her newly born pride. She *had* remembered the details and conveyed them with accuracy. Although her faint sullied it, up until that moment she'd handled herself well. Her heart twisted then, thinking how her father would be proud of her.

Penny worried suddenly that the last thought of his life may have been what others had voiced after his funeral, that his daughter wouldn't survive a day without him looking after her. Had he lost sleep over that, paced the parlor as Bentley now did, worrying what would become of her if she didn't marry before his passing?

"Maybe you should go check on her," the marshal

said, drawing her back to the moment. "If she's awake, I can talk to her before I leave."

"You've already questioned her until she lost consciousness, Marshal," Bentley accused. "She's been through a terrible ordeal, and the girl is not of a strong constitution. She cannot tolerate any more of your interrogation. She simply is unable."

Penny stiffened, ready to stomp downstairs and set Bentley straight. She'd taken no more than a single step when Bentley's next statement froze her in place.

"Thank goodness Penny's father was wise enough to make arrangements for her care."

"What kind of arrangements?" the marshal asked.

Bentley's shadow stopped before he said, "Well, he certainly couldn't leave all assets directly in her hands. She wouldn't have a clue as to how to handle her finances. In no time at all she'd be broke, squandering it all on bonnets and such."

Penny clasped the handrail and squeezed until her fingers hurt. Then she realized she was angry with herself more than she was with Bentley. After all, he was stating what he believed to be the truth, had no reason to think otherwise. The fact was her father *had* taken care of everything. But just because she hadn't handled the finances before didn't mean she couldn't. Did Bentley really think so little of her? Had her father?

"She seems like a capable young woman to me," the marshal responded. From her stance at the railing, Penny smiled through a haze of tears.

"You've known her less than an hour," Bentley pointed out.

"I'm a very good judge of character," Kincaid replied without missing a beat. "So what happens to her money, this house?"

"It's in control of her guardian, and that would be me, until she turns twenty-one or marries."

"When does she turn twenty-one?"

"Not for several months." Bentley's shadow took a step so he was standing directly before the marshal. "We'll be married by then."

Penny gasped, too outraged to care if they heard her.

"I didn't realize you two were engaged," the marshal said, his voice a tad more subdued. Penny resisted the urge to run downstairs and shout, 'We're not!' She wanted to hear what else Bentley had to say, and if he was aware of her presence, he might hold back. She suddenly remembered him at her house after the funeral, with the papers he had in his pocket. Was this the business to which he'd referred?

Bentley said, "Well, we *are* engaged, not that it's any of your business. Her father made the arrangements several months ago when he finally realized he'd spoiled her so badly she'd never settle on a man."

"An arranged marriage? You don't hear much of those things anymore."

"It was necessary. He knew I'd be good for her, trusted me to see to her care."

Pain the color of anger burgeoned inside her. How could her father have arranged things so, setting her up for marriage to a man she didn't love? Did he really think so little of her? Penny swiped at the tear rolling down her face. He did, everyone did, and maybe that was her own fault. Still, to leave her in such a position, she couldn't fathom it. Her father was fond of Bentley, had encouraged her to spend time with him. Had he been trying to prepare her?

"Oh, Papa," she whispered, and more tears flowed. "How could you?"

A moment later, she realized she wouldn't have to marry Bentley, after all. As he'd just told the marshal, she'd be twenty-one in a few months, and she would have full control over her money and her life. Until then she supposed he would make her live on an allowance. She wasn't overly concerned about any budget he might force upon her. It just grated on her, Bentley controlling her finances. But it wouldn't be for very long. She could certainly bide her time with polite manners until her next birthday.

"Congratulations," the marshal said, though it was mumbled and without a strand of enthusiasm.

At a knock on the door, Penny ducked behind the wall. She recognized Bentley's tight steps as he crossed the tiled foyer. A boy's voice said, "I have a message for Marshal Kincaid. Is he here?"

"Yes, this way."

Penny peeked around the corner to see Andy, Jo Ell Hanson's boy, walk through the door. Marshal Kincaid met him before he entered the parlor.

"I'm the marshal."

"The sheriff wanted me to tell you some bankers from St. Louis got together a five-thousand-dollar bounty for the capture of the man who shot and killed Frank Wills. Sheriff McElroy wanted you to know he rode out with a posse. He wanted to be sure I told you that." The boy of ten smiled then, enthused over the new turn of events. To him it was just excitement. "It was easy to gather up some men since there's a big fat reward. They're all sure they can find that no-account outlaw now that they know it's a man named Zeke Cotter. They'll catch him for sure."

"Damn it all to hell!" the marshal shouted before turning to snatch up his hat and coat from the rack.

On his heels, Bentley said, "You're going to stop the posse?"

"Those fools have dollar signs in their eyes and no leadership whatsoever to put any sense to their chase. I've got to find Zeke Cotter before one of your good citizens' ends up being his next victim as they're going after a man with a thirst for bloodlust. Worse than them getting themselves in trouble, they might go and string up an innocent man."

The marshal stormed out without bothering to shut the door. Penny stepped from behind the wall, staring down at Bentley. The movement caught his eye, and he looked up to see her.

"Penny, you shouldn't be up."

"I'm fine. They're going to catch him now," she said, her voice cool, her shoulders straight. "In the meantime, I have other matters to settle."

"Whatever do you mean? Penelope, were you listening to our conversation?"

"Yes, I was, and I'll tell you exactly what I mean," she said, marching to the stairs and then down, stopping when she was but a few feet away from him. "Tomorrow I'm going to see Papa's lawyer. I'm not marrying you, Bentley, and you're not controlling my money."

Surprise widened Bentley's eyes. Clearly, he hadn't expected this turn. He squirmed a little, as if literally searching for his backbone. In a calming tone, speaking to her as he would a child who didn't understand, he said, "It's already done, Penelope. Everything's been arranged."

"I will *not* marry you," Penny told him, angry at too many things to count. "I'll turn twenty-one soon enough, and then you'll have no say over me whatsoever."

Something hardened in him, then. Before her eyes, Bentley changed into a man she didn't recognize. A tremor of fear tore through her at the sharpening of his eyes, at the unfamiliar set of his jaw. He folded his arms in front of him and for a moment Penny thought she saw a hard smile touch the corners of his lips.

Bentley's voice no longer held a placating tone when he said, "You'll be broke by then."

"Broke? What are you talking about?"

"I'm saying if you don't marry me, by the time your birthday arrives there won't be a cent left in your accounts."

"You would steal from me?"

Bentley softened, then, as he took her hands in his. "I'm sorry for being so harsh with you, Penelope, but it's for your own good. And no, of course I wouldn't steal from you. You should know me better than that. By the time you turn twenty-one, the money will be in a separate account, one I will control. Upon your father's death, the property, this house, went into my name. That wasn't my doing. Your father arranged things so because he knew we'd be good together and you were just too stubborn to see it. I'd hoped not to have to tell you that part. No, don't be angry with your father. He was worried about you, Penelope, had been for some time now. You must have suspected."

Penny paced a few steps. The action reminded her

of Bentley, pacing around the marshal. She stopped immediately and faced him, head held high, hands on her hips.

"I'll hire a different lawyer, my own lawyer and fight you."

Looking pained, Bentley said, "You have no money to hire a lawyer of your own. Your father anticipated everything. He was a smart man, and he was well aware of your stubborn streak. I know it's a lot to take in right now, but you have to trust his decision. Your father knew what was best for you."

She looked into the parlor, as if her father would be there to tell her this was all a joke, or a misunderstanding. Then Bentley walked to stand before her, taking her hands in his. He smiled at her, looking shy and a little out of sorts.

"It'll be all right, Penelope. Your father knew it. Trust him. We'll be good together. You'll see. I'll leave you to think about everything, give you some time to adjust. Everything will work out. I'll be good to you, I promise. We'll have a good life together." And without waiting for a response, Bentley walked out the front door, closing it behind him.

With the weight of her circumstance slowing her steps, Penny made her way into the parlor where she could still smell her father's pipe tobacco. She managed to get to the chair near the window before her legs gave out. From there she watched Bentley walking in his brisk fashion toward the bank. After a moment, Penny put her face in her hands and cried.

Chapter 6

Garrett spent two and a half days on the road covertly trailing those hindrances on horseback. He'd endured temperatures too cold for this time of year, meager supplies since he'd had to gather them in a hurry, and a wind storm that liked to blow him all the way back to his family farm in Illinois. Adding to his aggravation, he'd not seen a single telltale sign that Zeke Cotter had passed this way. Garrett couldn't help but wonder if his instincts had turned fool on him.

He easily caught up with Sheriff McElroy and his sorry excuse for a posse. Not that it was any great feat. The men were raucous and disorganized, excessively ecstatic over earnings not yet in hand. If they thought they were going to sneak up on Cotter, they were as delusional as they were reckless. Of the nine men who rode with the sheriff, maybe three of them had any business being there, and that was a kind estimate.

The posse consisted of four wayward ranch hands, two of them young men with more enthusiasm than sense, but at least they had a working knowledge of guns. There were a couple of shop owners and one clerk, none of whom had likely ever faced anything more dangerous than a splinter. Adding to the farce, age had so stooped one of the shopkeepers, he looked like a skinny question mark, and the other was so sluggish and overweight Garrett felt sorry for his poor horse.

Topping off the group were a couple of saloon rats sobered up just enough to ride when they heard the news of the reward. Oh, and of course there was Sheriff McElroy, their unworthy leader who couldn't head a hunt for sunset.

It was the most pitiful posse Garrett had ever seen in his life.

Garrett watched last evening as Jeb, the man from the mercantile who traded his apron for an ill-fitting gun belt, got a shooting lesson from a cocky young man who left his barstool for fun and fortune. The kid was in sore need of instruction himself, or at least some sobering up. The only chance either one of them had of hitting Cotter with a bullet is if they got within spitting distance, and then threw the bullet at him.

Sheriff McElroy and some of the men had a few good laughs watching the two in their failed attempts to hit the fat trunk of a tree, a *tree,* while they passed around a bottle. Meanwhile, amongst the cowboys who had more experience with firearms there were grumblings about how they were going to divvy up the money. The four believed they were more an asset than the others were. They were probably right, and now their original deal of an equal split wasn't sounding so fair anymore.

The initial discussions of the posse as a whole had started a premature celebration. Everyone talking about what they were going to do with their cut. After two days living the hardships of life on the road, with their prize still not in sight, the celebratory mood was souring at a slow but steady pace.

Every one of them was now drinking. The more they all drank, the louder the grumbles from the gun-sure cowboys, and the responses from the others were becoming more irritated. All fingers of this group were pointing to trouble.

From the moment he came upon them, Garrett kept back, staying out of sight. He was hoping they'd tire of the deprivation and the elements and turn back before any of them ended up hurt or dead. Five thousand dollars was a hell of a lot of money, though. Apparently, sleeping on hard ground and eating what they'd hurriedly stuffed into their saddlebags or could find in the wild was not enough to deter them.

As much as Garrett wanted to make his presence known, order them all to turn back and let the law handle the matter, it was pointless. His threats of prosecution wouldn't stop all of them, if any. He'd been around enough to know if he tried, it would only get them all riled up and even incentivize the younger members into a heedless rebellion. They'd find a way to get around him. Besides, right from the start Garrett had a feeling his experience and instincts would eventually lead him in a different direction, in which case he wouldn't have to deal with them at all.

That would definitely be for the best. Even the men who knew how to handle a gun were getting no guidance from the sheriff. If Garrett tried to take over leadership, even if it was for their own good, they'd see him as an interloper, someone who could cost them a lot of money. None of them were taking into consideration in the least the man they were chasing was more desperate than ever. He was already going to hang for murder, so killing again would be nothing to him.

So, for the time being Garrett found himself in a

position of having to protect the posse. *Well, isn't this a fine state of affairs?*

The motley group was sticking to the main road, taking them westward. For all intents and purposes, it was a logical choice. The road connected several towns, a couple of them being large enough so a man could get lost, at least for a while. That Zeke Cotter was heading west was a reasonable assumption on their part. However, the outlaw may have realized that, too.

If Cotter headed south, he'd be entering denser terrain as opposed to land becoming more open where he'd be less able to hide. Food would be easier to come by and he wouldn't have to duck far into the woods should he hear riders approaching. For a long way, the towns would be smaller, but the trade-off might be a good one. Of course, if the outlaw wasn't thinking clearly, if he was just running with panic as his guide, well, then Garrett's theory was about as helpful as a good pair of oars on a sinking boat, which was exactly how it had begun to feel.

On the morning of the third day, his instincts proved right.

The crossroad wasn't much. There weren't any markings. The men riding a short distance ahead of him hadn't thought anything of it, if they noticed it at all between their weariness and their griping. Garrett saw it, though. And he didn't miss the single set of new horse tracks imprinted in the freshly blown trail. Cotter had a good head start, but if he believed that by going off the main road he'd lost anyone who might come after him, he could just decide to relax a little. He could even get it in his head to rest himself and his horse for a day or so.

Over the last few hours, the bickering of the tired men ahead escalated. Most of them weren't used to living like this. The days were long and tedious, the nights cold, and the ground a poor substitute for their beds. The group stopped at the top of a rise, only a hundred feet or so from the crossroad they'd missed where Garrett, concealed in a copse of trees, waited and watched.

From where he was, he couldn't hear what they were saying, but there was definitely a discussion on that rise. After a few minutes, Garrett circled around. Keeping to the thick pines off to their left, he saw what they were seeing, a good long stretch of open terrain. It was clear they'd lost their prey; at least it was clear to Garrett.

"Pleth is just about one more day's ride," one of the young cowhands said. "It's a decent sized town, and I'll just bet that's where he rode off to." The young man rubbed his hands together. "One more day to collect all that money."

"I suppose you're right," answered McElroy. His tone was agreeable, though it carried an undercurrent of doubt.

"If that's where he went," was Jeb's glum reply, scratching at the scruff on his face. "Who knows? He had a good head start."

"Yeah," the sheriff said. He rubbed his lower back and grimaced. "You're right. He could be anywhere by now."

"We just need to ride a little faster, that's all." This from the young man who couldn't hit a tree at twenty paces.

Suddenly, all of the men were talking at once, and

it wasn't long before tensions were on the boil. The sheriff was little help, changing sides each time someone made a new argument, though he clearly was ready to give up the chase.

Garrett turned around and left them to their business. Any minute now they'd split up, he guessed, some going home, some continuing in the same direction. Either way they'd be out of his hair. Once he got back to the road that hardly was a road, he turned his horse south and slipped away, glad to be rid of Sheriff McElroy's posse, hoping his instincts were right.

Less than five hours later Garrett had Zeke Cotter in his sights.

****

"Zeke Cotter," Garrett shouted with firm intonation. "You just climb down off that horse nice and slow and nobody has to die today."

The sun was close to setting, and Garrett had been just about ready to call it a night. He'd been tracking along a creek with clean running water and plenty of soft grass close by, two things both he and his horse would appreciate. It was a good place to wash and to sleep until morning. Then he could pick up Cotter's tracks again. He was pulling up on the reins to stop when a lucky star must have come out early, and beamed down upon him.

The shadow stretched out before him as soon as he rounded a short bend.

He snuck up on Cotter as the outlaw had remounted, fully taking him by surprise. No more than ten yards separated them. Garrett, sitting tall atop his horse, had his well-tended Peacemaker pointed line-perfect at the killer before Zeke even knew he was there. And it *was* Zeke Cotter he was about to take into custody. There was no doubt about it. After all the worry about the posse and the trouble they could wreak going after the wrong man, facing more danger than they were prepared to handle, or getting in the way of the law, it turned out this was going to be an easy capture.

Or so he thought.

Zeke jumped at the sound of Garrett's voice. He jerked his head, turning dark eyes toward the marshal, and then to the gun held in a steady grip pointed right at his chest. Fear, outrage, and frustration all crossed his scarred face in turn, as the man ran through his options, deciding which would rule.

"How'd you find me?" he asked, stalling.

"The law finds everyone, eventually."

Zeke slid a quick glance at his own six-shooter, still in the holster.

Garrett kept his gaze and gun fixed. "You'll be dead before you hit the ground."

After another second or two, Zeke wilted as his head gave a conceding nod. "All right, all right," he growled, holding out his hands. "Don't shoot."

For the life of him, Garrett would never be able to put in order the speedy succession of the next events. Everything happened in the time it took to sneeze. That's likely what kicked it off. Zeke Cotter sneezed.

Maybe the sneeze was fortuitous, or maybe Zeke decided to go for his gun after all and the sneeze was a ruse. Just before, Garrett's ears caught a sound behind him. An animal, possibly, but maybe his head turned the slightest. He just wasn't sure. It wasn't like him to take his eyes off immediate danger, but it ran through his mind if someone from the posse had followed the same trail, well, he could be sitting square in the middle of a shootout.

Garrett did see Zeke's eyes shift just before he sneezed, and he appeared to catch sight of something behind Garrett and to his left. Whatever set things off; Cotter made good use of the distraction.

The gunshot that followed Zeke's sneeze exploded in the silence.

All at once, birds took flight, bursting from the trees in a mad flapping of feathers and high-pitched screeches. The blast caused Garrett's horse to suddenly rear, which sent the unprepared marshal straight and fast to the hard ground.

Garrett landed flat on his back with the air knocked clean out of him. He lay there for a moment, dumbstruck, staring at a couple of lazy clouds pinned steadfast in an otherwise clear blue sky, and marveling at how abruptly the scenery had changed.

Dust rained down upon his face and he knew why. Zeke Cotter had turned his horse and was riding hard. Garrett closed his eyes against the grit. He then did a wary body check. Surely, he must have broken something. The way his body was screaming at him, he could have fallen from a second floor hotel room instead of his horse. It had been a very long time since a horse tossed him out of a saddle, years, many years. He couldn't remember if it always felt such a blow. At some tentative moves, he concluded nothing was broken, but he was sure as hell going to have some bruises.

Garrett suddenly realized his gun was not in his

hand. And someone behind him had fired that shot. Was it Zeke's partner, perhaps, who'd been waiting outside the bank that day? Maybe someone from that ridiculous posse had noticed the crossroad on his way back home and decided to give it a try. Whoever it was, Garrett needed to gather his senses and find his gun.

Lying perfectly still so he wouldn't alert the gunman in case it should be another outlaw, Garrett slowly opened his eyes. Instead of sunlight and sky, what filled his vision was a familiar face bent over his, and she was every bit as furious as she was beautiful.

"You let him get away!" she shouted.

"Penny?"

Garrett eased himself up on his elbows and took in the woman before him, not that she looked anything like a woman now. Except for a few wayward tendrils, she had all of her hair stuffed into a hat so old the right side of the brim sagged. She wore a boy's shirt and jacket, both faded brown. They matched the trousers she had on, tied at the waist with a rope. Garrett's eyes widened when he got to her shoes because those certainly belonged to her. The fashion boots were black, dusty, but still looked new, with fine laces and short, stubby heels that looked utterly ridiculous with the boy's attire. To top off the look, she held in her hand a Winchester. Smoke still coiled from the barrel.

"You had him, Marshal! And then you had to go and fall off your horse! And now…oh, are you all right, sir?"

Garrett dragged his gaze upward again until his eyes rested on her lovely face. She still had her brow furrowed, but no longer in anger. She was sincerely concerned for any injuries he might have. As she should be, since she was the one to cause them.

"Marshal, are you hurt?"

"I'm fine," he said in a tight voice, hoping it was true. Then her words sank in. "And I did not *fall* off my horse. I was *thrown*."

"Weren't you holding on properly?"

Did she really just ask him that? Before he could tear into her with the verbal lashing she wholly deserved, she was tugging on his arm trying to haul him up. When he didn't budge, she leaned back, putting all her measly weight into the effort.

"Well, if you're not hurt let's go. We can still catch up with him." She grunted with her exertion. "Come *on*."

Garrett stood. Not because her puny little arms were lifting him, but because he was afraid she'd hurt herself if she kept trying. Once upright, he bent at the waist and began slapping the dirt off his clothes. Not that he cared a whit about a little road dust. He needed the time to rein in his anger, which was wasting no time overrunning his shock.

Garrett's gun lay on the ground beside his now calm horse. He snatched it up and stuffed it into his holster before facing the woman who just scared him in more ways than he cared to count.

"Have you been following me the whole time?" he asked, even though he knew it was true. She hadn't just wandered all this way and come upon him by chance.

She drew a deep breath and blew it out between her pursed lips before answering. "Well, I didn't think you'd let me ride with you."

"You're damn right I wouldn't have let you come with me!" Though he was yelling at her, he was far more upset with himself. He'd been trailed for three days and hadn't a clue. He was a bigger fool than the sheriff's posse. How had she been able to do that? Damn! He was a lawman with a goodly amount of experience.

"Well see, there you go," she said easily, though there was a thread of wariness in her voice. "You didn't leave me any choice. I had to follow."

"Do you have any idea how dangerous it is for a woman out here alone?"

"I wasn't alone. You were a mere scream away."

"A mere…" Garrett wheeled away, trying not to think of all the terrible things that could have happened to her while he was 'a mere scream away'. He cocked his head in the direction in which Cotter had ridden off. A haze still hung in the air from dust kicked up by the outlaw's horse. After a couple of deep breaths, he turned back to Penny.

"Hurry, Marshal," she said, starting back to her horse. "He's not too far ahead of us."

"It's too late to track him tonight." Garrett snarled.

Penny turned toward the sun, sinking into the horizon. Darkness was already gathering around them. There would be a full moon tonight, and it would provide good light. She told the marshal just that.

"We can sneak up on him," Penny continued.

"Or we'll ride into an ambush."

Had Garrett been alone, he wouldn't have worried about such a thing. He would indeed have continued on, at least for a while, with the light of a full moon, especially since Cotter was so close. With Penny, though, the dangers were too high to count, and definitely too much to risk.

"So, we'll ride at daybreak?" she asked.

Garrett nodded his answer.

Penny brightened. "That's the spirit. He's not very far ahead of us. We'll catch him again for sure."

"We're not going after Cotter." He moved a step toward her. "As soon as morning comes, I'm taking you home."

She took a step back that was really more of a leap. "We've almost got him. You can't take me back now!"

"The hell I can't!"

"Don't yell at me, Marshal. You've no call, especially after I just saved your life."

"What! Saved my…"

"That man was about to draw his gun on you."

"My life was in no danger until you scared my horse right out from under me."

"I saw that. I would think a marshal to be a better horseman. Why, at The Boston Academy for Young Ladies, we learned all about good horsemanship. If you'd like, I could give you some tips."

All Garrett could do was stare at her, incredulous beyond words. What galled him most was her total lack of sarcasm. The girl was completely serious. Give him some tips!

Finally, between clenched teeth Garrett said, "We're going back."

"Sir, how can you even think about turning back now when we're so close to capturing that killer?"

"I'll see you safely home, and then I'll come back after him," Garrett said, taking a step toward her.

Penny took an equal stride back, hers much more of a stretch to cover the same amount of ground as Garrett's long legs. "Think of all the time you'll lose!

And who knows where he'll be off to by then. It could take you months to find him again."

How he wished she were wrong about that. By the time he got her back to Mill's Creek and returned he could expect Cotter's trail to lead him down many a false start. Now that Cotter was aware of the law being onto him, he'd turn every which way in an effort to lose his tail. Cotter could take up with a gang, or more likely, bury himself somewhere deep in the wilderness. There was always the chance the outlaw might wind up running into that inept posse of Sheriff McElroy's, and that was trouble just waiting to happen.

Still, the hardships of living on the trail and the dangers of tracking a killer was no place for a woman, especially a gentle woman like Penny Wills. He had to take her back, even if that meant costing him precious time. Garrett was about to issue his decree when Penny made a point as solid and as striking as a hard punch to the gut.

"In the time it takes you to find him again..."

Concern darkened her eyes, and Garrett knew why. In her mind, she was seeing the blood and the death, another funeral, the anguish of another loved one lost. He knew that's what she was thinking because he'd been there himself. She wanted justice, of course. She also felt the urgency, knowing full well every minute Cotter was free lives were at risk.

Snapping his gaze from her concern, Garrett stomped two long strides away from her. Then he spun around in the dirt. Penny was staring him right in the eye; she knew her point was good and valid.

Thrusting out his large hand, Garrett said, "Give me your rifle. You're a menace with that thing."

She hugged it close to her body. "I need it for protection."

"I need you *not* to have it, for *my* protection."

"Are we going then, I mean, after the man who killed my father?"

"Yes, and you are to do exactly as I say at all times. Do you understand?" He scooped the fingers of his outstretched hand a couple of times, flicking a meaningful glance toward the Winchester.

Penny's head tipped back as her eyes rolled toward the sky. If he didn't already have knowledge of her reckless behavior, Garrett would think she was on watch for the coming stars instead of evading his directive. But this woman had spent three days on the road, virtually alone. It made his teeth grind just thinking about it.

Garrett narrowed his eyes on her. "Either that, or I'm taking you home."

Letting her gaze drift back to earth, Penny gave him a speculative look. A moment later, she lifted her chin and then, begrudgingly, handed over the Winchester. "Very well then, take it. But I don't want to hear you complain if you need my help and I am unarmed, sir."

Torn between laughing and shouting, Garrett settled with, "One other condition."

"What's that?" Penny asked warily as he stepped much closer to her than necessary to collect the rifle. His hand gripped the long barrel of the Winchester just above hers, fingers against fingers.

****

At his touch, the oddest little quake rushed up her arm and through her body. Penny didn't have time to think about it, because that brazen marshal stepped closer still. When he finally stopped, there was scarcely room for a breeze to fit between them. It was really quite uncivilized. Yet, strangely, she found such closeness to him more exciting than unsettling.

Though Penny already knew the marshal was a big man, standing this close he towered over her. By all reason, she should feel intimidated, maybe even a little afraid, as his mood seemed rather dark. She didn't really know this man and after she'd made him good and mad she was now about to pass the night out here with him, alone.

Yes, she should be at least a little afraid. She wasn't though. For a reason she couldn't explain, Penny trusted him. Maybe it had something to do with him being more concerned for her safety than she was. While he'd been gruff, and had even become quite angry with her, he'd not threatened violence. She truly didn't believe he would harm her. But standing in such close proximity flooded her with other feelings she was struggling to understand.

The marshal moved his hand, then. His skin brushed against hers and that funny jolt shook her again. She looked at the Winchester as if to find a cause. Her hand looked pathetically weak beneath his strong grip. If he wanted to, he could simply take the weapon. But he was waiting for her to surrender it voluntarily. Would he take it by force if she did not? Likely, he would. He wasn't the bluffing type and for some reason he thought it was better if she didn't carry the rifle. So, after a just moment of consideration, she let go.

The marshal said something, and the deep timbre

of his voice sent another little quake rushing through her, setting a quiver to her lungs. What was it about him? She turned her eyes upward and regarded him. Dark whiskers, barely visible in the fading light, mesmerized her like a strange new animal. Penny found herself wondering what those whiskers would feel like against her fingertips. Tilting her head back a bit further, she raised her eyes to meet his. What little was left of the sun's rays shone at his broad back, shadowing the very masculine features of his face. He was looking right at her. Penny felt more than saw his scrutiny.

"Penny, did you hear me?"

"Um…what?"

"I said stop calling me 'sir'. My name is Garrett." He turned and walked over to his horse where he slid her rifle in with his gear. "If we're going to be on the road together, there's no need to be so formal."

"Fine." Her voice was a bit breathy, and she couldn't stop thinking about those whiskers. Why? It wasn't as if she hadn't seen facial growth before. Her father shaved every morning, but not all the men in town did. Several of them had full beards. Why did she find the marshal's whiskers so utterly distracting? She had no answer whatsoever, only a powerful desire to touch them. Whiskers, of all things!

Her thoughts weren't making any sense. She was just tired. That was it, of course. She hadn't slept well these past nights, what with all the sounds out there from the wild and no walls to keep her safe. She'd done it, though, without tears and without running to the marshal to protect her. The reminder bolstered her. Lifting her mood further was the fact that the marshal was going to let her ride with him. Together they would bring to justice the man who killed her father, and then she would collect the much-needed reward money. Her path to an independent life was off to a good start.

Lifting her chin, Penny said to the big man, "And you may address me as 'Penny'."

****

She'd already given him leave to do so back at the bank. Garret was about to remind her of that when he turned around to see she was smiling, not with arrogance, not with the haughty condescension that too often accompanies victory. It was just a smile, sweet and sincere. And when she turned it on him, eyes aglow with the kind of warmth that makes a man's breath take a pause, Garrett's heart beat just a little bit harder.

"I suppose we're friends now." She smiled even brighter.

In that moment, she could have asked him for the moon and Garrett would have figured out a way to get a lasso around it and yank it from the sky just to give it to her. Damn, if she wasn't pretty, even in that ridiculous getup she wore.

After forcing his gaze from her, Garrett lifted the hat from his head and used his other hand to brush back his hair. The ease with which he did so reminded him he'd just had it cut short. Replacing his hat, he said in a voice that sounded strange to his ears, "I'll take care of the horses. Start gathering firewood."

Garrett turned to collect Penny's horse. It was then he realized for the first time she had two horses with her. One, a brown mare with speckles of cream across her back and flanks carried her saddle and some gear, and the other, a fine chestnut with a thick blanket over

79

her back was carrying several canvas sacks.

Incredulous, he said over his shoulder, "Don't tell me you brought a wardrobe."

"No, of course not, silly, just a change of clothes. I was very practical. I only packed essentials, food, plates, utensils, soap, napkins, and such. Are you hungry? I have plenty."

Good God, the woman considered napkins on a manhunt practical? While that was beyond ridiculous, the thought of something to eat besides hardtack, jerky, and yet another can of beans made his stomach rumble. Garrett was indeed hungry.

"I could eat," he told her, and his stomach made another indiscreet sound as he wondered what kind of food she carried in those big sacks. He'd find out soon enough. It had to be better than what he'd been eating. "I'll take care of the horses first."

"I'll start collecting that firewood."

While Penny carried back armloads of twigs and branches, Garrett relieved the horses of their burdens and tied them near the creek where they could drink fresh water and eat sweet grass until their hearts were content. All the while, he kept an eye on Penny. It had been many years since he believed in fabled monsters in the dark, but every time she stepped too far into the deepening shadows of the woods, he found himself holding his breath, worried for her safety, until she walked out again.

A few minutes later, Garrett walked over to see she'd laid down first the smallest twigs and stuffed them with plenty of dried grass. She made a pyramid of the larger pieces of wood over the thick bed of tinder. Her ability to put together the makings of a good campfire was impressive.

As he searched through one of his saddlebags for matches, Penny carried over some more thick branches. "You taught me how to build a fire, you know. I watched you that first night. It was quite fascinating. I built one for myself, and it was very nice."

Garrett still couldn't believe he'd been followed and watched for three days and hadn't known, hadn't even sensed it. That was going to grate on him for a long, long time. Maybe she had an instinctive talent. Either that or he was losing his touch. He chose to believe she was a natural. *Hmm.* The thought almost made him laugh. Maybe she *could* give him some tips. He struck a match and moved the flame around the kindling until it took on all sides.

While he stood for a stretch and let the fire take, Penny dragged over two of her canvas sacks. From one she slipped out a red and white checkered tablecloth and laid it on the grass near the fire, smoothing out the wrinkles with her delicate hands as if laying it on a polished table instead of the ground. When the tablecloth met her standards, she sat upon it and began removing bundles out of the other bag.

Hungry awe wove through Garrett as she unwrapped each of the thick cloth bundles with care. Like gifts on Christmas morning, she revealed glass jars of tomatoes, carrots, and green beans, corn, and fruit preserves of some kind. It looked like strawberry. He hoped so. He loved strawberry preserves.

Simmering in anticipation, Garrett waited while she removed and unwrapped plates, *actual plates*, real silverware, and two checkered napkins that matched the tablecloth. Penny proceeded to dish out food for both of them with ladylike movements more appropriate for a tea party than a campsite, being far more generous with his portions.

"Oh, I almost forgot," she said, and then slid her hand into the sack again.

The cloth she unwrapped this time contained about a dozen fat biscuits. They couldn't be as soft as they'd once been, but they still looked to have plenty of give. She opened two biscuits and set them on Garrett's plate and one on her own before rewrapping the rest. She then dropped a heaping glob of fruit preserves on each. It was indeed strawberry, he saw.

"Dinner's ready," she said, after setting his plate down across from her.

She was looking up at him again with that smile of hers, the bright one that took his breath and left him feeling weak. Garrett's knees folded beneath him. It must have been the sight of all that good food.

"This looks wonderful, Penny. Thank you. Did you can all these?" he asked before shoveling in a mouthful of corn. The kernels were plump and sweet. He began spearing green beans with his fork before he'd even swallowed the corn.

Penny placed her napkin across her lap. She picked up her plate as she answered. "No. Pearl canned some of it. The rest are from the townsfolk who came to the house after the funeral. Just about everyone brought food."

Garrett nodded and tried the green beans. They were even better than the corn. "Who's Pearl?" he asked once he'd swallowed.

"She's our housekeeper and cook, well, main housekeeper. A few of years ago, Papa insisted she have someone come in a couple days a week to help. I borrowed these clothes from her. They belonged to her sons when they were younger. They're both grown and moved on now. I told her I wanted them to wear so I could work in the garden. She was happy to give them to me. Pearl has been with us since my mother died when I was seven."

He already knew she lost her mother young. It made the murder of her father that much more tragic. "Do you have many memories of your mother?" he asked.

"Oh, yes," she said, and gave him a catalog of events and details, too many and too clear for her to have garnered in the first seven years of her life, a couple of which she'd been too young to retain any memory at all. Her father must have told her the stories about her mother. So often that somewhere along the line, the accounts she heard turned to memories. It was clear to Garrett her father was indeed a special man.

Garrett nodded, listening to her precious stories while he devoured wonderful food off a real plate.

"Do you have any family, Marshal, um, I mean Garrett?"

"I have a younger brother, Seth, and a sister, Brianna. They live on the family farm back in Illinois with our mother."

As Garrett finished his dinner, he marveled at how ladylike Penny was able to eat sitting crossed legged atop a tablecloth spread on the ground. Even being dressed in Pearl's son's well-worn clothing couldn't deter from her femininity. She took small, dainty bites, her jaw working beneath that raggedy old hat. It was easy to picture her in one of those pretty dresses she'd handed out to the townswomen. He got curious then, about why she'd given away much of her clothing. Before he could ask her about that, Penny asked a follow-up question he wished she hadn't.

"What about your father?"

Garrett laid his fork on his plate. Just thinking about what happened to his father always made him lose his appetite.

"I'm sorry," Penny said after a moment. "Have I said something to upset you? Is your father a terrible person?"

"No, my father was the best a kid could have. He was kind and patient, a solid, reliable man. He was truly a decent human being. My father was the kind of man to step right up and help anyone in need. It's what got him killed."

Penny gasped. "Your father was murdered, too?"

Garrett nodded. He leaned back, raising one knee and resting his strong forearm across it. Penny set down her plate, waiting to hear the tale. He hadn't talked about it in years. Usually refused to, it still hurt that much. Before he knew it, though, he was telling Penny about his father's last day.

"We'd gone into town for some supplies, just the two of us. I was thirteen. A couple of half-drunk saddle tramps were harassing a young woman walking by herself. She was scared, intimidated by their size and brazenness. He told me to wait in the wagon, so I did. He walked over, real casual. I guess he was thinking just the presence of a man who would stand up to them would be enough. Men like that are generally cowards. My father said, in an easy tone, 'I think the lady just wants to pass, fellows.' I remember him saying that, kind of friendly-like."

Garrett stared into the crackling fire, seeing it all as clearly as if it was happening right in front of him all over again. "One of the men said, 'Supposin' we don't want to let her pass?' My father ignored that. I guess he realized there was no reasoning with them. He told the woman he'd walk her to her destination. She said something to him I couldn't hear and then pointed to a shop across the road. At first, it looked like those men were going to let it go. I remember relaxing back in the seat of the wagon. My father and the woman had walked about ten feet when one of the men drew his gun and shot him in the back. He died right there in the street."

"You saw your father murdered, too," she whispered. "Oh Garrett, I'm so sorry." Penny placed her hand atop his. "Being at the bank that day, it must have reminded you of what happened to your own father."

"Murders always do." He turned to look at her then, the empathy on her face lit clear by the orange light of the fire. Not many people could truly understand the way he felt about that day, the helplessness, the devastation, anger, immeasurable sorrow. Penny could, though.

"That was the day I decided I didn't want to be a farmer," he continued. "I knew I wanted to be a lawman."

"It's a terrible thing for us to have in common."

"Yes, it is. For me it was a long time ago." He turned his hand over and gave hers a squeeze. He liked the way her hand felt in his. Small, but there was strength running through her, sent to him in the return grip meant to give as much as receive.

"It gets easier, Penny. You don't ever forget, but it gets easier to live with." She lifted their clasped hands and rested her face against the back of his in a loving gesture that flowed deep in his chest. The fire warmed her face and the skin along her jaw was so soft Garrett wanted to turn his hand and touch it with his fingers. He didn't, though. He wouldn't take advantage of the kindness she was showing him.

"Thank you for sharing your story with me," she said. "I know it was hard."

For a moment, they sat unmoving, holding hands beside the crackling fire. The darkness around them could have stretched into forever. However, in their small circle of campfire light, with the glow of the moon silvering the creek beneath a blanket of glittering stars, comfort wrapped itself around the two wounded souls.

****

After a too brief moment, propriety separated them. Penny turned a shy smile to Garrett. He returned it with a grin and a wink before picking up his plate. A pleasant shiver washed over her. When the wave receded, it revealed a new burden.

Penny studied Garrett as he finished his meal. Now, on top of finding him physically attractive, on top of the respect he showed her, she learned they shared a common bond. That bothered her. She didn't want to feel any more drawn to him than she already was, not now. The timing was all wrong.

She turned away from him to stare into the fire. For the first time in her life, Penny was finding her own legs, and she feared that if she let herself get too attracted to this man, and if Garrett shared that attraction, she'd be surrendering those legs. She couldn't allow such a thing to happen. Especially now with her eye on new paths, down which she fully intended to make use of said legs.

Penny picked up her fork and toyed with it for a moment, then raised her chin to Garrett and asked, "Are you familiar with Susan B. Anthony?"

With a slight nod he said, "The Women's Suffrage Movement, of course."

She'd heard enough talk from the men around town who thought a woman voting was nothing short of ridiculous. Penny braced herself for a misogynistic answer, hoped for it, actually. She did not want to feel drawn to this man. An asinine comment from him on this matter would put her attraction to rest and she could better channel her thoughts where they needed to be at this time of her life.

When he just continued to eat, she said, "Well?"

He inspected the stewed tomato on the end of his fork. "Well what?" he asked before stuffing the tomato into his mouth.

She leaned toward him and said in a voice filling with frustration, "Women's rights."

He chewed. He swallowed. And then he simply replied, "Yes."

Yes. Yes, he agreed with them or yes, he heard her? She couldn't tell if he was being deliberately obtuse or teasing. Whichever the case, he had her worked up to a mood that bore little patience for either. He popped the last of his biscuit into his mouth, and Penny could swear she saw him smile while he chewed.

Irritated more than she should be, Penny said, "I

plan on joining the movement, and I was just curious about your opinion. What do you think about women having the right to vote?"

"If the fate of our leaders was decided by people like my mother and sister," he said around a mouthful of biscuit." He swallowed, licked his lips before saying, "The country would be a better place."

Her mouth dropped open just enough to draw in a gasp. Garrett supported a woman's right to vote. Her pulse picked up speed. Her heart swelled. He was handsome and brave and capable, *and* in support of women's suffrage. She was doomed.

With dinner finished, Garrett collected their plates and silverware and took them to the creek to wash. Penny focused on other tasks, carefully rewrapping the jars and putting them back into the sack, stuffing towels in between for extra padding. After folding the tablecloth, she took out some fine blankets and a pillow and made up her bed near the fire. Garrett brought back the dishes. Penny dried them and then, with the same amount of care, wrapped those, too.

Garrett was untying his bedroll when Penny said, "I'm going to the creek to bathe before I go to sleep."

Night had settled in, but the moon was full, giving them good light. "I wouldn't mind washing off some of this road dust myself," Garrett said. "You go first."

Penny gathered the things she needed. With a bundle in her arms, she turned to him. "I'm going to walk around that bend to have my bath. I won't be long."

"No."

"No?"

"Right here is fine."

"But sir…"

"Garrett."

"Garrett. It's…well…I would feel more comfortable if I was a little further away."

"I'm sure you would. Right here is fine." She opened her mouth to speak and he said, "That was the deal, if you remember right. You're to do exactly as I say."

"Yes, but…"

"But nothing. If you have trouble, I don't want to have to go looking for you. If you want a bath, you'll have it here." He moved then, turning his back to the creek. He slanted a sideways look her way with a grin that bordered on a smirk. "Call out if you need me."

Penny's spine stiffened, and she pursed her lips together for a good long moment before saying, "Very well" in her best clipped voice.

****

Garrett didn't know why, but ruffling her feathers like that made him smile from the inside out. Probably payback for all the trouble she'd caused. She spun around on those fancy little shoes of hers, and he turned back to face the fire. He heard her take two steps before stopping. Garrett knew she was glaring back at him because he felt it just as sure as if he could see it. Damn if he wasn't smiling again.

"Garrett."

After replacing his grin with a bland expression, he slowly turned his head around. Yes, she was glaring daggers at him all right. The corner of his mouth twitched upward.

"Give me your word," she said.

"My word?"

"Yes, that you won't peek."

For a moment, they just stared at each other. Then she raised one of her finely arched brows halfway up her forehead. The woman must have grown an inch stiffening her spine that way. Garrett had to press his lips together to keep from laughing outright. She sure was a prim little thing.

"You have my word. I won't peek while you're bathing." He then turned his back to her, picking up a twig to poke at the fire. Not more than a minute later, he was cursing his torturous honor. It may well have been more decent to just turn and look than to see the erotic visions his mind was showing. Try as he might, he couldn't help it. His mind stubbornly refused to see anything else.

Above the bubbling of the slow running creek, came the sound of her fussing with the bundle she carried to the water with her. There was a light thud. It had to be her old hat landing on the rocks. He wondered how long her hair was, if she was taking out the pins so she could wash it. Then he listened to the rustling of clothing as she stripped down for her bath. Garrett didn't move a muscle.

The last of her clothing must be off because those sounds stopped. She was naked only a few yards behind him. Garrett's body tightened and he tried harder to think about something else, anything else. He searched his head for another topic, but could think of absolutely nothing. He couldn't even think on the ridiculousness of that. All his mind could wonder at was what her breasts looked like, if they were as nice in the flesh as they were in his mind.

There was a small sound of displaced water as she

stepped into the creek. Right after, she gasped.

"Everything all right?" he called out.

"Yes, I'm fine," she called right back. "The water is just cold. Stay where you are, please."

He smiled again, and then had to shift his position as he pictured what the cold water was doing to those fine breasts that had taken up residence in his mind. Garrett blinked at the discomfort in his hand. The stick he'd been using to poke at the fire had itself gone aflame. The fire had almost consumed the stick and wasn't more than an inch or two from his fingers. Before the thing could burn him, he tossed it in the fire.

Garrett sat there listening to her little splashes. He remembered her saying she'd brought soap. The sudsy images that conjured caused him to scoot back from the fire. She'd built the damned thing too hot. Garrett tugged at his collar, feeling like he was about to go up in flames himself.

Finally, water dispersed as she stepped from the creek. That image stretched the boundaries of his sanity as he pictured her emerging from the dark water, her naked body glistening in the silvery light of a full moon. He had to scoot back from the fire some more. At this rate, in another minute or so he'd be sitting in the creek.

A few minutes later, Penny stood by the fire. Garret looked up and nearly choked on his own breath. Her hair was soaked, but she was doing her best to dry it with a nice, fluffy towel. It was long, he finally saw, almost touching her waist. Even dripping wet at night the color was as bright as sunshine. He was surprised he could take note of that at all, as his eyes were stuck on what she was wearing.

A nightgown, she was actually wearing a *nightgown*. A snowy white, somewhat wrinkled, lace at the wrists, white ribbon tied at her throat, nightgown! In all his born days, he'd never seen such a thing on the road. Of course, he'd never been on the road with a woman before. And, as he could see all too well, Penny was indeed a woman.

The garment was a bit on the thin side. He guessed that in her haste to be warm and covered she didn't realize there was enough dampness on her to make that nightgown cling to parts of her skin.

"If you go in the water by that big rock its smooth sand and won't hurt your feet," she told him, oblivious to what she was doing to his poor brain and body.

She faced him and leaned sideways toward the fire, rubbing her hair in an effort to dry it. In the flickering orange light, Garrett got an eyeful. Well, at least he now knew her breasts were as lovely as he'd imagined. Better, actually, from all he could see. Nature had been generous to her, more so than what he'd thought, considering she was a relatively small woman. He could see their dark peaks pressing against the white fabric of her nightgown, full and ripe in the cool night air. His mouth turned dry as the desert in August and Garrett could swear the blood rushed from his brain down to his more essential parts.

He should look away, he told himself. *Like hell!* He said he wouldn't peek while she bathed, and he hadn't. What was he supposed to do now, *not* look at what good fortune had put right in front of him? He was a man, not a saint. And she…she was a goddess.

Below her lovely breasts her waist curved inward and she had well-proportioned hips with just the right amount of flare. She turned her back to the fire, then, and crouched down to rummage through one of her bags. Garrett's hands ached to cup her nicely rounded bottom. In fact, it wasn't just his hands. He was aching all over.

****

"There it is," Penny said, sliding out her hairbrush. She turned around and sat down on her blankets to face the fire, sweeping her hair over a shoulder as she worked out the tangles. She hoped to get it at least close to dry before going to sleep so it wouldn't get her pillow all wet. Working from the bottom up, she took her time, savoring the warmth of the fire after her dip in that freezing creek water.

After a moment, Penny paused and looked at Garrett who was staring at her in the oddest way. "Aren't you going to bathe now?"

Garrett figured that was a real good idea. Of course, he'd have to spend half the night in that creek before he'd cool down. "Yes," he answered in a strangled voice, and then coughed to clear his throat.

As he walked away, Penny said, "Don't worry. I won't peek either."

Garrett laughed, but it was a painful mirth. He'd been right about something else, too. It took a good long soak in the cold water before he felt himself again.

She fell asleep before he did. It was a strange thing, sleeping so close to a woman with whom he hadn't had sex. It was a first for him. Frankly, he didn't much care for it. It was damned frustrating. He tipped his head back to have another look at her. She had curled up on her side, wrapped in nice thick blankets with her head on an actual pillow. She couldn't possibly be cold. He

93

sat up anyway, and tossed some more wood on the fire, just in case.

At some point, Garrett finally fell asleep. The last thought he had before he drifted off was that he was going to have to forbid her from bathing until they found a town and could stay at a proper hotel, in separate rooms, at the opposite ends of the hall. He chuckled then, even as his thoughts were sliding into dreams. If that woman was determined enough to have a bath, she would have it. Maybe he'd get lucky and the trail would take them away from the creek.

Chapter 7

"Let's ride," Garrett said, not that it needed saying. Penny was set to go before he was.

They'd both come fully awake before the first touch of sunlight had spread across the land. Penny slipped into the woods near the creek with a bundle in her arms and returned dressed and ready for the day in a matter of minutes. Breakfast was fast, biscuits eaten while they gathered their things. Garrett then secured her sacks to her second horse and checked once more to be sure the fire was out. He helped Penny mount her horse before climbing on his own. They were on the road before the sun cleared the trees on the horizon.

The air was cool, but the day showed promise. A cloudless sky helped the sun warm the land and signs of spring were beginning to show. Small, green buds appeared on the bare branches of oaks and elms, and wildflowers peeked from the tops of skinny stems, as if expressing a timid interest in showing their petals.

It was indeed a time for a fresh start. Penny tipped her head back, eyes closed, feeling the rising sun's warmth on her face. Her heart still felt shattered. She supposed it always would whenever she thought of her father. Maybe Garrett was right. Maybe time made it easier to live with. She could only hope.

She couldn't even begin to wish for such peace, until she saw the man who'd murdered her father brought to justice. Penny straightened her head, her hat once again shielding her face, and looked at the long road before them. How far ahead was Zeke Cotter? She wondered. And how long to find him? At their traveling speed, it was going to take quite a while.

They'd been on the road not more than fifteen or twenty minutes when Penny turned to look at Garrett who was riding right beside her. "Aren't we going too slowly?"

He nodded, though he kept his eyes on the road ahead, as well as the woods that thickened around them. Maybe that was her imagination. Maybe not. "We are. Can you hang on to that horse at a faster pace?"

"Of course I can. I told you, it was part of my education."

He smiled at that. "Ah, yes, The Boston Academy for Young Ladies."

"That's right."

****

Sliding a glance over Penny, Garrett took note of how well she held her seat. "I always thought those places taught young ladies to ride side saddle."

He was sure he saw a slight blush beneath the drooping brim of her hat. It galled him that he thought it was cute. He still wasn't ready to stop being mad at her.

"Well, yes, that's true." She gave a slight shrug of one slender shoulder. "But my friend Elena and I snuck away regularly and practiced riding astride."

Looking at her all decked out in boy's clothing, not to mention having firsthand knowledge of her recklessness, it wasn't hard to imagine Little Miss Refined indulging in an occasional fit of rebellion. For some reason that made him smile. Almost immediately, he forced it down.

"If I start to lose you, I'll slow down," Garrett said.

"I've kept up with you so far, haven't I?"

Garrett grinned, and let it be. He certainly couldn't deny her ability to keep up. However, he did have a hard time verbally conceding that fact. He picked up their pace a little. Penny kept up so well he picked it up some more.

They rode in silence until the sun angled between morning and mid-sky, at which time they stopped to give the horses a rest and tend to their own needs. The patch of woods through which they were riding had indeed become thicker. A man planning an ambush would have an easy time staying hidden.

Garrett walked the area at a slow pace, watching, listening, and even sniffing the air trying to catch a whiff of foul odor. His body moved as if merely taking an afternoon stroll. His eyes, however, roamed deep, continuously on guard.

A few minutes into their break, Penny said, "I don't see why I can't have my gun."

Garrett's eyes paused in their vigilance long enough to give her a direct look. "Because I don't need you shooting my head off while you're trying to kill Cotter."

Penny gave a slight shake of her head. "I wasn't trying to kill him."

"You weren't?" Garret asked, surprised. After his father's murder, he wanted nothing more than to kill the man responsible. He glanced off into the woods once more before turning back. His gaze shifted to study Penny's face. Her look of determination turned grave, and Garrett had the feeling it was an expression to which she was unaccustomed.

"No, I didn't want to kill him. To die in an instant like that is too easy for his crime. I want him to have to face a judge and jury for what he did to my father. He has to stand trial, all right and legal. Papa would have wanted it that way, too. I was just trying to wing him so he wouldn't kill you before you could arrest him."

Her chin rose then. Her eyebrows lifted and retreated just a tad over an expression that shielded her pride. Although he barely knew her, Garrett already recognized that look. She was about to say something that would make him want to simultaneously laugh and shout. He wasn't disappointed.

"My aim was only a tad off."

Garrett nearly choked on a huff turned guffaw. "If by a tad off you mean twelve feet, then yes, you were just a tad off."

Penny's eyes widened and her jaw dropped a bit before she put a fist against her slender hip. "My aim is *not* that bad."

"I'm only grateful you were off in the opposite direction of me," Garrett said low, under his breath as he turned his head away, scanning the woods.

"What's that?"

He turned back toward her. "Have you ever shot a gun before yesterday?"

"Yes, of course. Papa showed me once."

"Once?"

"Yes. On that very gun, as a matter of fact," she said, nodding to the Winchester now tucked in with Garrett's gear. "I was fifteen. I didn't care for the noise at all, but I remember everything he showed me. I have a very good memory."

"Good God," he mumbled, turning his horrified expression toward the woods. It was a miracle he was alive.

"What's that?"

He shook his head. "Nothing. Let's go."

They rode the rest of the day in silence. She had to be saddle-sore, not being used to long, continuous days of riding. When they stopped earlier, he'd seen her hold onto the saddle after she dismounted, trying to gain her legs. She didn't complain; he had to give her credit there.

When the shadows stretched long, ominous fingers eastward, Garrett slowed, allowing the horses to catch their breath. Soon they would stop for the night. That is, if he ever found a place that looked safe enough for them to stay until morning.

For the first time in a good long while, Garrett found himself wishing for a couple of extra men. Sleeping alone out in the wild had never bothered him. Hell, at this point in his life he probably spent near as many nights outdoors as in. Even while he slept, he had a keen sense for danger. Suddenly, though, he worried about sleeping too soundly to protect Penny should Cotter decide to circle back and eliminate the threat.

The road Cotter had taken branched off into at least a dozen different directions and so far, Garrett hadn't lost the trail. This situation with Penny, however, blanched that satisfaction to almost nothing. It seemed no matter where they stopped for the night, they'd be easy pickings. The worry was growing as tall as their shadows.

Garrett cast furtive glances everywhere. His ears turned his attention to every sound. Keeping the pace slow, he began what suddenly seemed an impossible task, finding a safe place to spend the night. They'd passed a dozen spots that would have suited him just fine, had he been alone. Today, though, no place seemed safe enough.

Once, open spaces, especially with the light of a good moon as they'd have tonight, eased his cautious nature with a full view. Tonight, they left him feeling exposed and vulnerable. Instead of wooded areas giving him peace of mind with a series of alarms such as twigs that would crack if stepped upon, or dried leaves that would rustle when kicked, all he saw were places for a killer to hide. Again, he worried his sleep would be too sound. Or, he would have just one careless moment. That hadn't been a concern for many a year.

Peering into the gathering darkness, Garrett's mind flooded with horrific possibilities.

In the dwindling sunlight, as they rode beside the creek that swelled to fair-sized, Garrett questioned the saneness of allowing Penny to come with him. Every time the wind blew or a squirrel twitched its tail, he had one hand on his gun and the other ready to grab Penny from her horse and toss her to the ground. After hours of riding at high tension over mounting concerns, his nerves were beginning to ache. Every instinct he had told him this had been a mistake.

"Penny," he began.

"I'm not going back."

He raised a brow at her. "How did you know…?"

"I see the way you keep looking into the woods, like the devil himself is about to pounce at any moment."

Garrett brought his horse to a halt. Penny stopped

beside him, her shoulders straight, chin high, ready for a fight. As much as he admired her fortitude, now he wished she had none.

Garrett glanced off into the woods, vigilance wearing him thin, before turning back to face her. "The devil *is* out there somewhere, in the form of Zeke Cotter. This isn't going to work, Penny. I can't hunt down a killer and babysit you at the same time."

Penny threw him a withering look. "Babysit! Did I ask you to babysit? Do you think that's what I expect? I'm sick of people behaving as though I couldn't so much as bathe myself without somebody watching to see that I don't drown!"

Emotion crept into her voice. "I know it's my own fault." She sniffed back the tears, but more rolled from her eyes. "All my life I've let Papa and Pearl take care of everything for me. Now, because of my own self-imposed ignorance I have nothing!"

"Nothing? Penny, you're upset and not thinking clearly. You have a fiancé, and I'm sure Bentley will take good care of you."

"Bentley is not my fiancé!"

Garrett felt a loosening around his heart at that news, though he'd have to analyze that later. Right now, all he could think about were the tears filling her eyes, and how when they spilled down her face it twisted his insides. He had to squeeze the reins to keep himself from scooping Penny into his arms and holding her on his lap.

"I was under the impression you two were to be married."

"It's what my father had arranged," she said, with angry swipes at her tears. "He was worried about me so he put everything in Bentley's name so I would marry him. He meant well. But I don't love Bentley, and I just can't marry a man I don't love. That's why I can't go back without Cotter."

"I don't understand. What does one have to do with the other?"

Penny then told him the idea that had formed these last days on the trail when she'd had nothing for company but her thoughts. "I can give piano lessons, and etiquette lessons. Young ladies for miles around can get the benefit of my education for a fraction of the cost. I'll make my own way in this world, just like Coleen O'Conner did after her husband died."

Again, Garrett looked at her with respect. This world held few opportunities for a woman to survive by herself, and some of those were downright unsavory. Penny had found a way to take what she knew and use it to make a life. He found himself grinning at her, as he marveled at her fortitude. No doubt about it, Penny Wills was a woman to admire.

"I'll show everyone I can do just fine on my own," Penny continued. "See if I don't. All I need is a little seed money to get started, and the reward I'll collect after capturing Zeke Cotter is it."

Twisting his head away from her, Garrett swore under his breath. After a moment, he turned back to see her sweet face, so full of pride and determination. It killed him, knowing he was about to crush her well-laid plan to dust.

"Penny…"

"What?" she asked with a delicate sniff. From the pocket of her hand-me-down jacket, she withdrew a lace-lined handkerchief and dabbed at her face.

"I'm arresting him."

"Yes. So?"

He drew in one long breath and told her. "I'm a Federal Marshal. You can't collect the reward if I'm the one who takes him into custody."

For a moment, Penny sat utterly still, utterly silent. Then she shouted, "But that's not fair!"

"I'm sorry, Penny. I truly am. That's the way the law works."

"Well, the law isn't fair! I've been riding and searching, just the same as you."

"I know."

"I even brought a gun!"

Garrett gave her a smile too full of compassion to hold any laughter. "I know. Look, maybe an attorney can help you with the way your father left things. I have a name or two I could give you."

Penny deflated before his eyes. She'd been struck with one too many blows, the last taking her to the ground. She turned away from him and stared across the creek at nothing. Water rippled onward in a dull shimmer beneath the last vestige of light. It was near to full darkness now, in every way.

With little conviction, she said, "Maybe an attorney could help me."

Garrett shifted his eyes to glance at the horizon. Shades of night had a chokehold on what was left of the daylight. They couldn't ride any further. Not that it mattered. At daybreak, they'd be turning back. Garrett shifted in his saddle before saying, "We'll make camp here tonight. Tomorrow we'll head back to Mill's Creek. And Penny?"

Though she said nothing, she did turn to look at

him. The despair in her eyes clutched his heart. "I *will* catch the man who murdered your father," he promised.

She answered with just a nod.

They ate a quiet dinner, speaking only when necessary. After making up her bed, Penny gathered her things for another bath. Garrett turned his back to the creek. She didn't complain and he didn't tease. He found himself missing her chafe at their banter. She bathed quickly and when she was done, he took his turn to wash off the day's dust. When they finally climbed into their makeshift beds and said goodnight, the words they'd spoken since making camp totaled less than a dozen.

Tired and road weary, they both fell asleep before long. Garrett awoke to her whimpers.

He looked over to see her eyes closed and her body restless beneath the blankets. He waited to see if her nightmare would pass. When it got worse, when he heard the fear in her quiet cries, he rounded the fire to lie beside her and take her into his arms. She turned into him as if it were perfectly natural. It felt natural, holding her as he was. With a gentle touch, he placed his hand on the back of her head and drew her close to rest against his chest, whispering to her, trying to soothe her. It worked because she did settle.

Once she was calm, his brain told him it was time to go. Just a minute more, just to make sure her nightmare didn't return. That's what he told himself. By the time the third minute had passed, he was already adept at ignoring that voice of sanity.

The problem was it didn't just feel natural to hold her, it felt *right*. Penny's small hand had come to rest on his chest. Her head tucked beneath his chin where he could smell the rose-scented soap she used on her soft hair. Her body fit nicely into the curve of his. In fact, fit in perfect form. He bargained with himself to stay no more than another moment or two while his honor and his desire debated the accurate length of a moment.

Garrett knew the instant Penny awoke. Her body stiffened, and he was sure he'd frightened her with the intimacy of his presence. But when he drew back from her, Penny's hand clutched at his shirt. Her head tipped upward, and he looked down to meet her gaze. The firelight caught in her wide eyes, giving radiance to the emerald color. Her skin was sleep-flushed, looking soft as a fairy wing in the glow of the moon. She spoke her words in a quiet voice. The pull of them, however, was as strong as a locomotive.

"Stay, please. Just a little while longer."

Garrett answered with a slight nod. For several moments, they looked into each other's eyes. The green of hers mesmerized him, how the color gleamed iridescent, as if she had swallowed all the stars in the sky and their light now shone from within her. Then he wasn't thinking at all. He didn't even seem to be acting from his own mind but rather, from instinct so primal he could have been a caveman laying stake to his claim.

As his head bent down to kiss her, Penny raised her lips to his.

She was inexperienced, he could tell right away. But Penny's eagerness more than made up for her lack of skills. For a long time, their kisses were little more than a mere brush of the lips. Then Garrett touched her lower lip with his tongue to see how she'd react. Instead of being repulsed or afraid, as was his concern, she moaned from the back of her throat and moved closer to him. As he explored beyond her lips, she opened for him, and with a move sweetened by its awkwardness touched her tongue to his. It so aroused Garrett, his honor was shredded and left to float inertly in the far-off peripheral of his desire.

Penny tasted him once more. Her own response amazed her, awakened her to feelings she'd never known and could never have imagined. His hand was on her back, large, warm, drawing her closer. Still, she couldn't seem to get close enough. When his hand moved down her back to cup her bottom, pulling her against him in a most intimate fashion, wondrous sensations exploded within her, taking over her body, as well as her mind.

Garrett dragged his hand up over the lush curve of her hip, further, until it rested against the fullness of her breast. She gasped and pressed herself into his hand. Impassioned, he kissed her again, more thoroughly, as his fingers teased her taut peaks. Eager to feel her bare skin, Garrett bent low enough to grip the edge of her nightgown.

Penny couldn't speak, couldn't think. She seemed only to live and breathe for his touch. When her nightgown whispered up her legs, and his hand slid along her thigh, a small part of her thought to tell him to stop, that this was improper. But she didn't want him to stop, ever. Propriety be damned, it felt too good having his hands on her body. All she wanted was more.

Garrett dragged his hand along her soft, warm thigh and let it rest on the swell of her bared hip. Her skin was as velvety as the rose petals with which she shared a scent. He moved to taste her neck, her throat.

With an airy sigh, she tipped her head back to allow him what he wanted and in that moment, Garrett wanted it all.

His hand slid to the inside of her thigh and inched upward. When he touched her, she cried out, gripping his arms, her small fingers digging in. In moments, she was writhing beneath him. At her climax, she buried her face against his neck, her cries of pleasure the sweetest thing he'd ever heard.

She lay beneath him then, warm and breathless. Garrett's breath was heavy, too. Near to bursting from his clothes, he leaned back enough to unfasten his trousers. She turned her head toward him. Garrett kissed her, astounded at how hungry he was for this woman.

"I love you, Garrett," Penny whispered against his lips.

Garrett froze. It was certainly not because he wanted to. Penny was unlike any woman he'd ever known, strong, brave, and she was as elegant as a princess was, even wearing her boy's clothing. He could spend a lifetime getting to know all of her parts, inside and out. But he could not take her virginity like this. She didn't understand the ramifications. Probably didn't even understand her own feelings. She was innocent and vulnerable and for the duration, completely dependent on him. He would not take advantage of her. With far more will than he felt, Garrett stood and refastened his pants.

"I'm sorry," Garrett said. After he finished righting himself, he looked down at her. Her passion had turned to embarrassment. No, it was worse than that. Shame dulled her eyes that wouldn't quite meet his as she sat up and wrapped the blanket around her.

Garrett opened his mouth to speak. A better apology was in order, much better. However, the right words just weren't there. Frustration strained his body. His heart and head were as spun as a wagon wheel at full speed. He needed to explain things to Penny. Things like not confusing lust for love.

He turned away and shoved both of his slightly trembling hands through his hair before looking back to her again with every intention of making her understand. The problem he had is that it wasn't all that clear to him, not while the heat of a passion he'd never before felt with a woman was still running through him. He needed time to think. He needed to manage his words before he spoke to her.

"We'll talk in the morning," Garrett told her, his voice gruff with unsated need.

She nodded and lay back down, turning away from him and curling up on her side. For the first time in his life, Garrett wished he were more like his brother, Seth. Seth always had his nose in a book and was good with words. Garrett, on the other hand, did his most important talking with fists, and sometimes with his gun. He would sleep on it. In the morning he would talk to her, apologize for his behavior. Once outside this new experience, Penny would see her feelings weren't real.

Garrett attributed the ache he suddenly felt poking at his center to his unquenched desire. He'd feel better tomorrow, too.

Satisfied with his plan, he walked back to his bed and lay down. He rested his head in his hands as he stared up at the stars. For a long time he remained awake. He thought Penny was awake, too, but he let her be. He wanted to have the words right before he spoke to her so he wouldn't make a mess of things. By morning, he'd know just what to say.

At some point while he was running conversations through his head, Garrett fell asleep. When he awoke, Penny was gone.

Chapter 8

Penny slowed her horses to give them another chance to rest. When she first snuck away in the middle of the night, the darkness forced her to ride slow. Once the morning gave her the first glimpse of light, she rode hard taking intermittent breaks so as not to strain her horses, Lulu and Lady Bell.

Twisting about, Penny had another good look around. Everything appeared normal. It was another cool but sunny day and even though the brightness bothered her sleep-deprived eyes, she was glad for the light. Garrett's vigilant watch for danger had rubbed off on her. No matter her other feelings for the man, she wasn't so stubborn that she'd not learn by his example.

From the moment she left, Penny had kept a sharp watch of her surroundings. Zeke Cotter was out there somewhere. Maybe he was on the run far away, or maybe he was coming back to kill the witness he now knew was following him. As the day ticked on, that second possibility took on weight.

Her bravado began to wane in the hours since she'd snuck away, knowing full well this time she was truly on her own. Well, she was just going to have to gather it up again. She refused to turn back. Pride, however, was poor company, and a sorry protector. Never before in her life had Penny ever been so completely alone.

For the first three days after she left Mill's Creek,

she had the illusion of being alone. Penny had to admit, sleeping outside by herself, even though the marshal was not far away, had been a bit frightening. All kinds of unidentified noises rooted through the night and even with her small campfire, darkness engulfed her. But the experience had also been liberating. She made decisions, choosing her own course of action and following through. Besides, as she told Garrett, he was close enough to hear if she screamed.

That first night she walked low over small hills, weaved through trees, and hid herself in the brush and evergreens to see how he did things, learning how to live outside. She watched as he tended his horse with a gentle pat and murmured something to the great animal. The horse raised his head and nickered, as if conversing with the marshal. He said something else to the horse. She couldn't make out the words, but the tone was kind and she found that utterly endearing.

For a large man, he moved with grace. She'd studied him as he collected wood for his fire, tossing thick logs as if they weighed nothing. All of his movements were smooth and easy. He was probably a good dancer. The music and colors of a barn dance played in her mind. She imagined herself twirling in his arms, and sighed.

He cocked an ear then. Penny held herself as still as the shrub behind which she was crouched as he scanned the darkness. Her sigh couldn't have made any more noise than the breeze against the pines, but he'd picked up on the tiny, misfit sound. Penny silently cursed herself. Her silly schoolgirl daydream could have ruined everything.

After a long minute or so, the marshal returned to

what he'd been doing. Penny observed with a student's eyes as he cleared an area of fallen branches and leaves. He then made a small circle of rocks in the space he created. He picked up some dried pine straw and dead leaves and put them inside the circle. Upon that, he laid quite a few twigs. Then, over the kindling, he used the larger branches to build a pyramid of sorts. He struck a match to light the kindling and in no time, he had a wonderful fire. It was fascinating. Penny couldn't wait to go back and build one of her own.

She watched as the marshal untied a roll and then made up his bed near the fire. Next to that, he placed his hat. He removed his coat and after folding it, put it at the end of his makeshift bed. Oh, he was going to use if for a pillow. What a clever way to save space when traveling on horseback. Here she'd gone and packed a pillow from her bed.

The marshal stood then and stretched, arms raised, muscles pressing against the fabric of his sleeves, testing the buttons over the hard surface of his chest. Penny's eyes widened. She'd never seen a man like him before. He was magnificent, strong, handsome, and confident in his dangerous line of work. The man really was straight out of a dime novel.

He then turned from his fire and walked over to the creek. As he unbuttoned his shirt, Penny's eyes slammed shut and even though she couldn't see a thing, she still turned her head away. She'd gotten what she'd come for, a lesson in building a campfire. That was simply a necessity, she told herself, so it didn't really count as spying. So why did she continued to crouch there in her hiding place instead of making her way back to where she left her horses?

In her head, she heard Miss Mable's voice, the head mistress back at The Boston Academy for Young Ladies, preaching respect for the privacy of others. Penny had gotten the lecture after Miss Mable caught her and her friend, Elena, eavesdropping on two teachers discussing a fellow teacher's dismissal on the grounds of 'immoral indications'. They were beyond curious as to what immoral indications were. Before they could find out, however, Miss Mable caught them with their ears pressed against the door.

It took a good deal of apologizing and promises not to listen to other people's conversations ever again before Miss Mable agreed not to notify their parents of what they'd done. Elena's parents would have been furious. Penny's father would have been disappointed and she thought that was worse. The two of them spent all of their free time over the next two long weeks mucking out the stables as their punishment.

So, after that Penny made a great and successful effort to mind her own business. Eavesdropping was a bad habit. One she thought she'd shaken, until she listened in on Bentley and the marshal when they were speaking in the parlor. Of course, if she hadn't listened in, then she wouldn't have learned of the problems she faced until it was too late.

All right, in that instance eavesdropping was forgivable. But this grievous invasion of privacy was not. Yes, Penny told herself as she huddled in the darkness with her eyes closed, she had to leave, immediately. No question about it. Then, just short of enough propriety to stop, she opened one eye. She was staring at a tree trunk. Penny turned her head back, and with a silent gasp, opened her other eye.

The marshal had taken off his shirt, and she stared as he turned her way to hang it on a tree branch. Penny nearly swooned. She'd never before seen a man bared so. At that moment, she thanked her lucky stars the sun had not yet fully set.

Garrett Kincaid was, quite simply, beautiful. Dark hair sprinkled over the sculpted muscles of his chest, not an ounce of fat on him, not a hint he was anything less than perfection of the male form. When he turned away from her and knelt beside the creek to wash, Penny stretched her neck further to gaze at the muscles playing along his broad shoulders. After scooping water into his big hands, he splashed his face and torso. She stared through tight breaths as rivulets of water streamed down his sinewy back.

The marshal stood up then and unfastened his pants. Having pushed her affront to decency to the very limit of her courage, Penny turned around and with the swift stealth of a field mouse, scampered back to where she'd left Lulu and Lady Bell.

What she had done then, once she caught her breath, was build her own fire just the way he had. She made her own little campsite, which she accomplished quite competently. She was proud of how she handled herself ever since leaving a note for Pearl that her friend Elena had come with her brother to collect her so she could stay with them for a little while.

That is, until last night.

In light of what happened between them the night before, Penny was glad she had not confessed how she'd watched him past learning how to build a campfire that first night. As it was, she had enough humiliation to last a lifetime.

She'd acted as if she possessed no morals whatsoever. Of course he'd been repulsed by her. Penny felt her face burning in a blush thinking about how she had behaved. And then to tell him she loved him! Even if it felt real, she shouldn't have come right out and said it, not after knowing him such a short time. And for her to give her body over to him so easily the way she had, no wonder he turned from her as if she was dynamite with a lit fuse. What on earth had come over her?

Penny considered her feelings for Garrett again. She'd known him such a short time. Yet, the attraction she felt for him was unlike anything she'd ever experienced. Good lord, she even found his shadow attractive! That thought made her laugh as she recalled the sight of Bentley pacing around him downstairs in the parlor like a nervous mouse before a lion.

Garrett was certainly a fine looking man, in a rugged and rough sort of way, yet still beautiful, she thought as she recalled his bare torso. The whole of him made her think of Zeus, formed of strength and beauty, the mythological god of, among other things, law, order, and justice. If she remembered right, Zeus also had a rather amorous nature. Thinking of how Garrett made her feel last night, well, she figured that aspect suited him, too.

What captured her heart, however, was the way Garrett gave credence to her words and opinions. When she spoke he listened, really heard her. And his attitude was so progressive. My goodness, the man actually supported women having the right to vote! From just the little he'd said about his mother and sister, Penny found herself wishing she could meet them. His parents had certainly done a fine job.

Garrett worried for her safety, but he never made her feel inept. All right, well, except in regard to her shooting skills. In all fairness, it was entirely possible her aim *could* stand just a bit of improvement. On every other front, though, he treated her as no man or boy ever had.

Garrett spoke to her mind. Not only did her wants matter to him, but also her thoughts. That's what struck her now. That was the elusive quality. The one she'd been waiting for. It was what none of the young men back home had ever been able to give her. That was the reason she'd not been attracted to any of them. Not one of them had ever shown her a level of attentiveness that extended beyond the superficial.

And those kisses! Bentley kissed her on the cheek before. And once, during a barn dance, Jimmy James dared to kiss her square on the lips. Both times she felt nothing, nothing at all. With the barest touch of Garrett's lips to hers, every caution and every moral ingrained in her throughout her entire life flew right out the window.

Then, she'd gone and told him she loved him. Those sacred words leapt from her mouth without bothering to check first with her brain. The memory of his reaction had her cringing all over again. The man had been less offended when she shot her rifle in his direction!

At least there was one silver lining to her dark cloud of shame. Now she could catch Zeke Cotter on her own and collect the reward money. Without looking, Penny patted the Winchester she had reclaimed before sneaking away, wishing she had more experience with the thing. That was something else she would add to her list of things to change. Once she got everything settled, she would practice shooting until she was proficient.

So lost in thought, Penny didn't realize she'd entered such a heavily wooded area until the denseness of her surroundings fully engulfed her. Beyond the heavy growth, she could hear the creek, but she couldn't even catch a glimpse of the running water. The air became noticeably cooler. Goose bumps rose along her skin, and she couldn't completely attribute them to the temperature.

Giant pines, branches full of green needles grew into one another to form walls of inescapable denseness. She cast an apprehensive glance upward. Strung to tall maples, a multitude of dry leaves had managed to hold on through the winter, keeping out much of the sunshine, as did the substantial evergreens. Even where the light managed to break through, it was only speckled and supplied less than sufficient illumination against the thick gloom.

All around, the shadows multiplied. Then suddenly, the woods sprang to life.

A rustling of leaves to her right made her start. Penny had her Winchester out of its holder and pointed at the direction of the sound. She breathed a sigh of relief as a squirrel leapt past and scampered up a tree. A moment later, she tensed again at what she could have sworn was a footstep behind her. She swung her gun around. Nothing was there but Lady Bell, her packhorse who plodded along without a care in the world.

She was being overly cautious, maybe even a little paranoid. Or maybe not. Just then she caught a ghostly flicker of shadow from the corner of her eye. But when she turned to look, nothing was there but the melding trees.

The dim setting had a menacing feel, but in reality, Penny didn't see anything out of place. Yes, it wasn't unreasonable to think Zeke Cotter could be out there, hiding, waiting for just the right moment. She was, after all, a serious threat to him. Maybe he was taking aim at her right now. She peered through the varied layers of shadows, all of which she felt encroach in a menacing fashion as soon as she turned her head away.

A sharp gust tore through, blowing around the trees to run in cold breaths across the tender skin of her face. Penny had to hold her hand atop her hat to keep the sudden upsweep from yanking it from her head. The wind snatched leaves from the ground, giving them a clattering swirl and kicking up loose dirt before settling down again to a mild breeze. The subsequent silence pressed in. The darker forces of nature exhaled in relief, as if closing in on what they sought.

Penny pulled back on the reins until her horse stopped. She rotated her head and body with great deliberation so she could get a good look in every direction, and then she did it again. Nothing appeared to be amiss. Yet, a tingling crawled up her spine and she wondered if that was intuition, if Zeke Cotter really was close, following, watching. Given the opportunity, he would kill her for sure. She waited. She listened. Everything was as it should be.

Scolding her overactive imagination, Penny rode on. Sporadic sounds drew her attention, movement over long-dead leaves, a footstep, a breath, even. Every time she looked, nothing appeared out of the ordinary.

Sitting stiff in her saddle, Penny couldn't ignore the ache rooting itself in her neck and shoulders. She made an effort to relax before her tense muscles brought on a headache. *Be vigilant, not paranoid.*

Less than an hour later, Penny needed to relieve herself. She reined in her horses and took another slow look around. It seemed there wasn't another soul in the whole world. Again, the hollow of Garrett's absence stung her, and she wished he were riding beside her. She missed his conversation, even missed debating his occasional high-handedness, but she especially missed his company. Penny shook her head and brushed all that away. A woman had to maintain some measure of self-respect.

After sliding the Winchester back into its holder, she dismounted and found a bit of privacy. It was silly to think about such a thing as privacy when she was out here all alone, but she couldn't help it. Living outdoors as she had the last few days was still new. She returned to Lulu and ran her hand along the horse's sleek, muscled neck, deciding to allow the animals to graze a bit more while she walked around and stretched her sore, stiff muscles. She should get into her bag and have something to eat, but too many knots tied her stomach to think about food. Instead, she paced.

Her mind drifted back to Garrett. She probably should have left a note for him, a basic courtesy. But once the idea to leave struck, her emotions latched on and carried her away in every regard. Not that it mattered. Even if she thought of it last night, she had no means with which to leave one. Besides, how would she even begin such a note? "I'm a shameless woman with no morals and I've fallen in love with you"?

And how did that happen anyway? She wondered again. How does a woman fall in love just like that? Penny leaned back against the rough bark of an elm as her horses nibbled on some sweet grass.

She made a complete fool of herself. Of course, Garrett had been a complete cad. Yes, he absolutely had. She nibbled on her lip and frowned. Just because he didn't love her back, he still should have said something nice, at the very least said he cared for her, that she was lovely and smart or some such thing to buffer the insult. He certainly should not have turned away from her as if she was something slimy he'd discovered when he flipped over a rock.

Penny shoved away from the tree and paced, anger overwhelming her shame. Garrett had no reason to be so rude. A true gentleman would have at least offered some frilly words to mask his distaste for her, given at least a pretense of politeness.

Penny released a long sigh. She didn't want a pretense. She wanted a man who would behave honestly, and Garrett had done just that.

Suddenly, shame called her a coward for having fled the way she had. No matter her feelings, it wasn't right to leave him in such a way. His advice had been sensible. What she should do is get the help of a lawyer. Surely, her father had left some sort of opening for her. He wouldn't have locked her fate with such finality. He loved her. He cared for her. Her papa would never have arranged things with the potential to leave her without financial support.

Penny stood beside her horse, stroking Lulu's long fuzzy nose while accepting she'd have to go back and handle this situation like an adult. Besides, Garrett was probably worried about her. No, there was no probably about it. Even if he cared naught for her feelings, Garrett took his responsibilities seriously. He was certainly frantic searching for her, and guilt nibbled at her for causing that. She had several hours head start. It would be a while before he found her. She could turn around and meet him halfway. Yes, that's what she would do.

"You little bitch."

Penny jumped and spun around, shocked at the words as much as the unfamiliar edge in which he spoke them.

"Bentley?"

Penny couldn't believe her eyes. Bentley Werner was the last person she expected to see way out here in the wilderness. She took in his disheveled appearance, stunning because that too was something she had never been a witness to before. The man was never ever anything short of impeccably dressed and well groomed. For goodness sakes, he kept a cloth in a drawer at the bank for dusting off his shoes. For a moment or two, Penny wasn't even sure it was indeed the same man standing before her. He looked like Bentley's evil twin.

His hair was dirty and mussed. Days of uneven growth patched the dirt on his face. Dust covered his wrinkled clothes. Several snags looped out to mar his fine jacket and a long tear rent the fabric near his waist, leaving a ragged flap hanging. A deep scratch across his forehead had scabbed over, and two smaller ones on his right cheek stood out bright and angry against his fair skin.

What truly struck her, though, was the furious

display of his countenance, the malevolence radiating from his eyes, but above all that, the gun he had pointed right at her chest.

"Yes, it's Bentley." He sneered, his rage barely contained. "Well, at least you remembered my name, if not your place."

"What on earth are you doing here? How did you find…Bentley, why are you pointing that gun at me?"

"Because I'm going to kill you, you little fool."

Penny started to ask why, and then it struck with the impact of a vicious slap. She knew why he was going to kill her. She also knew, in that dizzying moment, that Bentley was somehow involved in the death of her father.

"You were part of the robbery." She breathed the words. Though she held no doubt it was true, Penny didn't want to believe the man her father mentored, had trusted with his business, was the one to orchestrate his murder.

"So you're not as empty-headed as I'd believed. More's the pity. Even though the proof is right in front of me, I still can't believe you charged after him, Penelope. You're even more out of control than I believed. We all thought you'd gone to stay with a friend from school."

"I left a note saying so," Penny said, speaking from a daze. She just couldn't reconcile the meek man she knew from back home with the crazed monster now standing before her. "I didn't want anyone to worry."

"I wasn't worried," he replied with disdain. "Privileged people like you always land on your feet. I was aggravated that you left without consulting me first."

Penny started to ask why he thought she should consult him before she did anything. But of course, it was because Bentley had already begun to live as if they were betrothed.

"When I saw you a moment ago, dressed like that," he said, looking at her boy's outfit with an equal mixture of shock and disgust. "I knew one of us had lost our minds. Fortunately, it was you."

"Why, Bentley? How could you do such a thing?"

Bentley ignored her questions as his gaze hardened, and then climbed back up to her face. "You've caused me a lot of trouble, Penelope. It appears my luck is changing, though, coming across you like this. I've been riding like the devil, off the trails and through every branch and bramble trying to get to that clod of an outlaw first. No one has any respect for a well-thought out strategy," he mumbled through his tight, thin lips.

"No matter," he continued, focused once again. "I'll catch up with Cotter, and believe me I'll deal with that imbecile. Then I'll stay a night or two in West Bend." He nodded down the trail. "I deserve a decent hotel after what I've been put through. I still can't believe you remembered such detail about that miscreant. Frankly, I'd expected you, not Neil, to faint as soon as you realized you were in the middle of a robbery."

Penny stared at him, too furious to be afraid, too stunned to speak.

Bentley's eyes focused on Penny again. "I planned that day right down to the last detail. It was a perfect plan, too, until that idiot Cotter proved just how inept a man could be. Letting his face get exposed," Bentley muttered. "And then he's so anxious to kill, he forgets to take the money from the safe! How does somebody so stupid live to adulthood?"

Looking at him with utter dismay, Penny said, "My father was good to you. He taught you everything he knew about banking."

"Your father was a bigger fool than you."

Penny gasped.

"Having more heart than head is no way to run a business. Giving people loans he shouldn't, granting extensions. Why, I once saw the man accept garden vegetables as payment. No, they didn't even have the vegetables to hand over yet because it was almost a month before they were ready to harvest!"

Penny knew about the incident to which Bentley referred. It was yet another action of her father's that made her so proud of him. That act of kindness was just one example of why the people of Mill's Creek loved and respected him.

"The Brewsters were going through a difficult time," Penny told him, her chin high. "Papa was going to buy their vegetables anyway. He worked it so everybody got what they wanted and needed."

"Banking isn't run on the barter system, Penelope. Frank Wills made a mockery of the business."

Penny glared at him. "My father never arranged a marriage between us. He never signed those papers at all. You forged his name."

"No, Penelope, your father signed them. It's all right and legal." Bentley scoffed then. "He trusted too easily. It was nothing for me to slide the papers I wanted him to sign in with some others. All I had to do was to wait until he was preoccupied," Bentley said before taking a step toward her.

"And you." He spat his fury, only slightly doused with disappointment. "I would have permitted you a fair allowance, though nothing like what your father foolishly lavished upon you. You could have lived out the rest of your days in the house you've always known, lived a comfortable life."

"As your wife," she said stiffly.

"Well you've ruined that now." He sneered, lips peeling back from his teeth for a moment as if he might bite. "Why must I always suffer fools?"

"You don't love me any more than I love you. Why would you want to marry me?"

"Love? Love is for fairy tales. Life is a business. I find your appearance pleasing. You're well mannered, educated, and your social skills are up to par. We could have had a good life together, Penelope."

Bentley paused then, while his gaze made a slow and lascivious voyage over her body. He slipped the gun into his coat pocket and took another step in her direction, stopping within a breath of her. Quick as a snake, he clasped her jaw in his hand, anger radiating from each finger. She jerked back but he firmed his grip, squeezing until she whimpered. An evil grin boasted his pleasure. Penny looked into his eyes and saw the future. Bentley was going to kill her.

His eyes held not a trace of the dedicated and somewhat shy man she'd known. The man who stood before her now was heartless and brutal; a disciple of evil who had her father murdered. Then the truth of it all hit her with the force of a lightning strike. The Bentley she'd known had been the grand façade. All along, this was the real man.

"Now we only have today," Bentley said in a voice that dropped to a low chill.

Penny twisted from his hold and stumbled. Panting short breaths, Bentley caught her, his fingers digging into her shoulders until she cried out. When he forced his open mouth over hers, Penny wrenched herself back far enough to slap him across the face. Instantly, he reddened with rage. His eyes hardened with violent intent. He drew back his arm and his hand slashed through the air, striking her with enough force to throw her to the ground. Before she could roll away, Bentley was on top of her.

"No!" she screamed as he tore at her clothes. "No!"

Her fists pounded anywhere she could hit, and she struggled to get out from beneath him, but his full weight was upon her. Bentley lifted his hips high enough to get a grip on the waist of her trousers. Her fight grew fiercer, more frantic. His chest pressed down hard against her and his legs were on either side of hers, effectively trapping her. Penny screamed at him again, and was sickened at his expression of ecstasy her struggles evoked.

Then suddenly Bentley's head jerked back at a sharp angle and he was facing the sky. His mouth gaped and from it burst forth a high shriek of terror and pain. Another sound reverberated through Bentley's screams. The rolling, vicious growl of an animal arose from the fray like an avenging demon straight from Hell.

Whatever the thing was, it dragged Bentley backward and off her.

His legs kicked, his arms flailed, and his fingers grasped at the air. Then, whatever had him, let go. Bentley curled up in a ball near her feet. It was then

Penny saw the dog, skinny, but ferocious, and worked up into a frenzied attack. Its brown and black hair stood on end and it snarled, barked, and growled, snapping bites with its bared teeth, chomping at Bentley as if it meant to chew him to bits.

The ripping of fabric rent the air. At Bentley's loud wail, she lifted her head enough to see the dog sink its teeth deep into the man's thigh. With his free leg, he managed to kick the beast away. Bentley struggled to get to his feet, half-crawling, part leaping in an effort to get away, but the dog jumped up and used its teeth and legs to fling him back down to the ground.

The dog shoved his head under Bentley's coat and latched on to another piece of his shirt. Skin, too, she was sure, from the pain in Bentley's shrill cries. She sat up just as the dog flung its head from side to side, coming away with a scrap of Bentley's bloodstained shirt in his teeth. It was then that Bentley managed to dig the gun out of his coat pocket. He turned and fired, the shot blasting the air and echoing through the woods.

The dog let out one terrible cry and stumbled back. Bentley used the opportunity to scramble to his feet and point his gun again, this time taking aim. But the dog lunged at him before he could shoot. In his stumble back, Bentley dropped the gun.

He kicked at the relentless dog and landed a foot in his furry chest, shoving the animal away long enough for him to jump on his horse. The snarling dog leapt toward him, his teeth piercing Bentley's calf. Bentley screamed again, trying to jerk his leg away, pounding at the dog's head with his fist. The dog let go and fell to the ground. It rolled, just barely far enough away so the horse did not trample it in the frenzied escape. Bloodied and terrified, Bentley was screaming still even as he disappeared into the woods.

Penny sat stone still in the sudden quiet as the animal gained its feet and turned its head toward her. For a moment she was petrified, waiting for it to attack her as it had Bentley. However, it no longer looked like a vicious beast. The dog actually appeared shy as it dropped its head and, panting, limped over to where she sat. She stiffened, but when the dog got to her side, he simply sat before her.

After a discreet peek, Penny said, in her most placating tone, "Hello, boy."

The dog whimpered and she saw a line of red where the bullet had grazed its left hindquarter.

"Thank you. You saved my life," she said in her most soothing voice, still gaging the dog's temper. The animal certainly seemed calm now. In fact, she could hardly believe it was the same animal that just a moment before looked as if it would kill.

With a tentative hand, Penny gave him a soft pat on his head. She was relieved when the dog pressed its furry face into her palm. It was such a sweet, loving gesture. On top of winning her gratitude, the dog now claimed her heart.

She leaned over and had a look at his injury. The scratch wasn't too deep, but it was bleeding. "Don't worry, boy. If you'll trust me enough, I'll clean your wound for you. I have some salve with me that will ease the pain."

On shaky legs, Penny managed to stand, and then to walk. She untied one of the bags from Lady Bell and carried it over to the dog. After carefully cleaning the wound, she applied the salve and then wrapped his leg in a cloth. The blessed thing was patient all the way through her ministrations. He didn't fuss or nip at her, even when she knew her gentle touch hurt.

"Good boy," she said when she was finished, scratching him behind the ears. The dog leaned into her hand and gave her a slow blink, a look of bliss on his furry face. Penny giggled. "You like that, huh? What in the world is a good dog like you doing out here all by yourself?"

She wondered if someone had abandoned the dog. Sometimes people did things like that. The very notion of such cruelty made her furious. It was also possible its owner had died out here somewhere. He'd belonged to someone. The dog wasn't feral. He didn't know how to hunt down food for himself. The poor thing looked like he hadn't had a decent meal in a good while.

"Are you hungry? I'll bet you are." Penny retrieved her other bag from Lady Bell and started opening jars. The dog watched closely, sniffing the air every time she twisted off a lid. He licked his chops, sniffed some more, but waited as if minding his manners. Then Penny and her hero dog sat on the ground and ate a quiet lunch together.

"You're the one who's been following me, aren't you?" Penny said as she used her fingers to pluck a stewed tomato from a jar. She tore it in half, the larger of which she fed to the dog. Fortunately, he wasn't a picky eater. The dog licked its chops as she tore a piece off a biscuit and fed it to him. They were getting stale, but he didn't seem to care.

"Poor baby, wanting company, but too afraid to approach, is that it? You sure got brave when I needed you. I owe you my life, um, hmm. Well, I can't call you dog. You're going to need a proper name." Penny thought for a moment. "I know. I'll call you Frank, after my father. He was brave and smart, too. How does that sound?"

The dog gave her a contented blink of his soft, brown eyes that made her smile. "I'll take that as a yes. Well, Frank, we'd better get going. I think we'll ride on instead of going back. From what Bentley said, the town of West Bend probably isn't too far ahead. We'll be safer in a town, too. The marshal will find us there. Besides, I would dearly love a decent hotel room for the night. How about you, Frank? I'd like to have a real bath. And, if you don't mind me saying so, you could use one, too."

The dog replied with an airy woof, showing no offence and making Penny smile again. "Well then, that settles it."

She secured her bags of supplies to Lady Bell. Then, holding the dog in her arms, Penny managed to climb up on Lulu without jostling the poor, injured animal too much. Frank sat tall and proud in the saddle in front of her, looking as if he was the leader. Penny stroked his furry neck and when he turned his head back, she could swear he winked at her. She giggled and then gave him a scratch behind the ears. Penny got her horses into motion, and with Frank keeping watch in front, started toward the town.

Chapter 9

Garrett could not make his brain believe what his eyes were seeing. He squeezed his eyelids shut for a cleansing blink, thinking the sun must be affecting his vision. He already knew his sanity was under attack due to the maddening worry over Penny being out here by herself, with Zeke Cotter somewhere in the area. Making things worse was the cold fear that had washed through him when he'd heard that gunshot a while ago. He'd ridden like the wind trying to catch up to her.

Yes, between his lust, his fury, and his fear, Garrett was sure Penny had scrambled his brain and it was now playing tricks on him. He certainly couldn't have seen a dog riding a horse.

However, when he opened his eyes, Garrett found the same sight he'd rode upon just a minute before. Penny was riding her horse at an easy pace, her packhorse following close behind. The woman he wanted to both hold close to know she was all right and at the same time shake until she swore an oath to never to scare him like that again, was riding along the trail that had opened up to a broad meadow. A dog was sitting in the saddle before her.

Garrett sat there for a minute or so before riding up to her. For one thing, his horse needed the break. For another, well frankly, so did he. Every nerve ending on his body still felt like needles erupting from his skin.

After hearing that gunshot, he pushed his horse as hard as he dared. The whole time his heart pounded a tempo to beat the animal's hooves as the worst possibilities ran through his mind in vivid detail. After filling his lungs with a few deep breaths, Garrett took his horse at a slow pace toward the woman who'd scared several years of his life right out of him.

By the time he got close, Garrett did a fair job of reining in his unruly emotions. Whether or not they stayed in place was still yet to be determined. At the sound of an approaching horse, both she and the dog turned. Penny had her Winchester out at an impressive speed. The dog lowered his head, laid his ears back until they were flat against his head, and growled low in his throat, showing teeth he seemed all too prepared to use.

"Garrett!" she said, turning partially toward him as she patted the dog, giving him a pleasant smile, as if they'd come across each other at the canned goods section of a mercantile. She slid the rifle back into its holder.

"Penny," he replied tightly. He would have shouted, but the dog looked like he'd leap over and tear his throat out if he did. He'd ask about the mutt later. Right now, there were matters of greater importance he had to settle.

In order to pacify the dog, Garrett kept his voice down, but he gave Penny a glare that had cowed many a rough man. He was too angry to see it had no effect on her. "You must have turned half the hairs on my head gray with that stunt," he told her, surprised the words could form within his tight jaw.

Penny lost her smile immediately. Instead of

bowing her head for an apology, however, she turned up her nose. "That wasn't a stunt. I've pulled stunts before and I can assure you, that was not one."

The dog growled again and Garrett, not knowing what to say to such an absurd response, gave a pointed nod at the dog. "Where did that raggedy beast come from?"

"He is not a raggedy beast," she replied, sounding as if he'd given her a personal insult. Running her hand down his furry back, Penny said, "He's a hero and a fine dog."

"Well, tell him to stop growling at me," he said, expecting her to give a command. What he got was an introduction.

"Frank, this is Garrett. Garrett, Frank. It's all right," she said to the dog, as if Garrett's presence was the one needing an explanation. "He's a friend."

As if the dog actually understood what she was saying, he relaxed a bit. However, he did keep his watchful, brown eyes on Garrett.

With one raised brow, Garrett said, "Frank?"

"I named him after my father." Penny rubbed the dog under his chin and laid her cheek against his big neck. "He's very, very brave."

Noticing the bandage around the dog's back leg, Garrett asked, "What happened to him?"

"He was shot in the leg."

"You shot him? *Damn*, woman, I said you were a menace with that gun!"

"Don't be ridiculous. I didn't shoot Frank. Bentley did."

"Bentley?" Garrett said, as a cold feeling suddenly crawled up his spine.

Penny nodded, her head tipped toward the dog. "Yes, Bentley. Frank here saved my life. Why, if this heroic dog hadn't come along, well, Bentley was going to…he'd nearly…" Penny turned her face into the dog's fur, hugging him with trembling arms as it all caught up with her. Frank bent his head and licked her hand.

"Penny," Garrett said with quiet prodding. "Tell me what happened."

And so she did. Near the end of her telling, she turned to face him. That was when Garrett saw the swelling on her cheekbone, a bruise already coming to color. His teeth ground together and his hands balled up into tight fists in anticipation of what he was going to do to Bentley Werner once he caught up with him. He'd not get away with this.

When Penny finished her story, Garrett had the urge for a comforting lick to the hand from Frank, with a whiskey chaser. His calm demeanor was a façade. Inside he was raging a temper the likes of which were unequalled by anything he'd ever felt before. Oh, yes. Bentley would pay.

"Are you all right?" he asked when he could trust himself to speak without his fury showing through.

"Yes," Penny answered while stroking the dog's fur as if it was a talisman. "Thanks to Frank here, I am." After a quiet sigh, she bent her head so it rested against Frank's neck. "Since all the documents are legal, signed by my father, Bentley now has my house and all of my assets as well."

"What he did was deceptive, especially in light of what's happened since those papers were signed. He's a criminal, a killer, and a swindler. I know a good lawyer who can help you set things right."

"Thank you," Penny said, though her dispirited tone reflected her doubt. She sat up and scratched Frank behind his ears. "Certainly Bentley will deny everything he said. He only told me because he was sure I wouldn't be alive to repeat it."

Without realizing it, Garrett's fingertips brushed the butt of his gun. Just thinking about Bentley having his hands on her, moments away from killing her, and the horrible thing he would have done to her first, had him envisioning Bentley in his sights. He didn't want to shoot that waste of human skin, though. He wanted to beat him to a bloody pulp.

Garrett looked over at the dog and wanted to buy him dinner at the nicest restaurant in town. The dog was looking at him, too. His solemn brown eyes appeared rife with noble intellect. An understanding passed between them, as they sat as equals upon their horses. Garrett was grateful, and it was as if the dog fully comprehended that fact. Frank's ears perked up. His shaggy tail wagged, and Garrett could swear a smile played at the curve of the dog's long mouth. Garrett let his hand drift over, slow, unthreatening, and gave the dog a scratch. Frank rewarded him with one of his loving licks.

Back to business, Garrett turned to Penny. "I'll arrest Bentley right along with Cotter. Cotter will testify against him, and you won't have anything to worry about."

Penny looked at him then. "Do you think he'll do that?"

"If it means going to prison as opposed to the gallows, he will." Of course, he'd have to catch up to them before Bentley killed Cotter, which was certainly his plan. Probably it had been all along. After what Bentley had done, with all he had to lose if Cotter talked, Garrett figured killing the outlaw had been in Bentley's plan from the start. Before he could do his job, though, he had to see to Penny's safety.

"Oh," Penny said, slipping a hand into her pocket and taking out Bentley's gun. She handed it over to Garrett. "Bentley dropped this. It'll be much easier to catch him now that he's not armed."

"Penny, we've already been over this."

"I'm going after them, too," she said, her stubbornness showing through. "I think I've proven you can't stop me. Besides, I need that reward money now more than ever. Even if you're right about what a lawyer can do, he won't work free, and I'll need money to live on in the meantime. As you said, I won't get one penny of the reward money if you catch him before I do. So listen, I have a plan."

"I can't wait to hear it," Garrett mumbled.

Annoyed at his sarcastic tone, yet nevertheless undaunted, Penny said, "You go after Bentley, and we'll catch Zeke Cotter."

"We?"

"Frank and me. Don't roll your eyes at me, Garrett Kincaid. Frank has proven himself to be a worthy partner."

"Penny, I'm not going to argue this."

"Neither am I."

"Look what just happened." His voice rose. "It's too dangerous."

"It's a lot less dangerous now. Not only do I have my Winchester, as I've just pointed out, I have Frank. He's the best protector in the world." She turned apologetic eyes up to the marshal's then. "Not that you aren't very good, too, Garrett," she added.

"Thanks," Garrett said, disgruntled over the way she placed his ability to protect her second behind a dog. The fact that so far the dog had done a better job chafed the insult sore. He turned his scowl toward Frank who sat tall and regal in the saddle, as if fully knowing his worth. Garrett released a conceding sigh. The dog *had* saved Penny from a terrible fate. It didn't change things, but he was indebted to the animal.

The dog actually lifted his scruffy chin, and Garrett could swear Frank looked down his long nose at him. He would have laughed at the arrogant beast if the situation hadn't been so serious.

"Before we go," Penny said, bending around to look at Frank's face, slanting only a brief look in Garrett's direction before turning back to the dog. "Frank and I both need a moment of privacy."

Garrett dismounted while trying not to smile at her discreet way of making her needs known. If he smiled, she might think all was well, and it wasn't, so he kept a tight face. He took the dog, careful of the animal's injury, and squatted until Frank's paws were on the ground. Even though she didn't need his assistance, Garrett put his hands around Penny's waist and helped her dismount, holding on longer than necessary. He set her down on those fancy shoes that were a comical incongruity to her raggedy, hand-me-down outfit. If he lived to be a hundred, he would never forget how she looked in that getup. He damn near gave in to a smile again.

The feel of her narrow waist in his hands gave him an inexplicable joy. Relief probably inspired that, he figured. He'd been worried sick since awakening to discover she'd run off. Just moments ago, after what Penny told him about Bentley, he'd been furious. Since then, as if it had been so long ago, she'd butted heads with him, vexed him with her stubbornness, and now she had him wanting to smile like a silly schoolboy. This woman constantly sent his emotions every which way.

As he watched her walking into the woods on her low-heeled shoes, her boy's trousers snug on the enticing roundness of her hips that swayed with womanly grace, that mangy, heroic dog trotting along beside her; it occurred to Garrett a man could lose his balance with a woman like her. Yes, he most surely could.

It was just a few days ago, he'd been thinking about settling down with a nice, stable woman. That was only minutes before he met her. What he'd envisioned was not Penny Wills, with her headstrong ways and her willfulness. Damn it, though. He stared across the greening, sun-flecked meadow. It was certainly her now. How could he fall for a woman who seemed hell-bent on making him crazy?

He remembered his father once saying something about losing his balance when dealing with his mother. They'd had an argument. Garrett had been about eleven or twelve. When he asked his father what was the matter, he said sometimes that woman made him lose his balance. Then suddenly, Garrett clearly remembered, his father's anger was gone. His father and mother looked at each other across the table where she'd been rolling out dough, and they both busted out laughing. Then he hugged her and she gave him a kiss on the cheek. Garrett still remembered her flour handprints on his father's back. All he'd thought at the time was that his parents could be silly to the point of embarrassment in their love for each other. And that he couldn't imagine ever getting that daffy over a woman.

Yanking off his hat, Garrett shook his head. That was more than enough of this nonsense. Once this situation was finished, he could figure out what he was going to do about Penny. Right now, he had serious business before him, and he had to get his brain in order. Garrett slapped his hat back on his head and paced the wild meadow.

While his mind worked, he glanced off toward the woods. Penny was right about one thing; she wouldn't be cowed into following his orders. His mother would appreciate that kind of fortitude. Maybe he would too, in another circumstance. Right now, he needed her to submit to his command. She wouldn't, though. He knew it as surely as he knew his own name. The woman was stubborn enough to do what she wanted and he couldn't take the chance of her running off again. He wouldn't.

Garrett was going to have to take drastic action. She was going to be mad as a pestered hornet, but he didn't care. He had to protect her, and he sure as hell wasn't going through the kind of frantic worry he had today. Especially now that he knew not only was Cotter a danger to her, Bentley was, too.

Garrett reclaimed her Winchester, took it over to his horse, and secured it with his things. He then rummaged around in one of his saddlebags for the item he was going to need. As he held it in his hand, he stood torn between a wry grin and utter dread. His feelings didn't matter, though. Penny's safety did. He took a few steps toward the woods and stopped, feet planted, hands behind his back, and he waited.

A minute or so later, Penny walked out, her trusty dog beside her. The dog's tail wagged in time with his steps. Only a slight limp showed he had any discomfort. Garrett's expression must have given him away because her face grew suspicious as she approached and her steps slowed.

"Penelope Wills," Garrett said in his professional voice.

"Yes," she answered, stopping in a field of caution.

Stepping right up to her, he said, "I'm placing you in protective custody."

"What does that mean?"

With movements that were both rapid and efficient, Garrett had the rope wrapped around her waist. Fortunately, Penny's attitude toward him had relaxed Frank enough so he could do it without upsetting the dog. In fact, the animal hopped around a little, barking once in a playful matter, as if they were all enjoying some sort of game.

"It means for your own good you aren't leaving my sight."

"What! What are you doing? Stop that!" she said, swatting uselessly at his hands.

Once he secured the knot at her belly, Garrett scooped Penny up in his arms and carried her to her horse. He dropped her in the saddle and then tied the other end of the rope around the pommel of his own saddle.

"Are you…is this like…like you're arresting me?"

"Like."

She gave the rope a hard tug, but the knot was too secure to budge. "Cut this rope off of me, right this instant!"

"No."

"You can't do this!"

Without a trace of regret, Garrett said, "Yes, I can."

"That's not fair!"

"Not entirely."

He handed the dog up to her, who settled into his place before her in the saddle. She then turned a hostile glare on him. When she opened her mouth to argue, he met her glare with his own. "Penny, Zeke Cotter wouldn't think twice about shooting down a woman, and you already know Bentley Werner wants to kill you, especially now. Hell, he confessed to you what he did. You could send him to the gallows, at the very least, to prison. As far as the reward goes, well, I am sorry about that. I have some money put away. I can help you."

"I don't want your money or your help! Untie me, you, you tyrant!"

"No," Garrett said and he climbed in his saddle. "And stop trying to untie that knot. I'm being nice. It would be easier for me if I just used the handcuffs."

"Handcuffs! You wouldn't dare!" She plucked at the knot with vicious swipes, then, out of frustration, yanked at the rope a couple of times, all to no avail. At the sound of clinking iron, she swung her head toward Garrett.

He had her attention now, dangling the iron cuffs in front of her. "I would, and I will. Don't push me, Penny. This is for your own good."

Her chest heaved, and she stared daggers at him. "I

hate you, Garrett Kincaid."

He turned away from her and got the horses moving. Slipping the handcuffs into his coat pocket, he said, "At least you'll be alive to hate me."

Neither of them spoke another word until they rode into the town of West Bend. It was larger than Mill's Creek, but hardly a city. It had what they needed, though. Garrett gave the place a cursory glance as he brought the horses to a stop in front of the Sunbird Hotel. The white paint on the boards was fresh. Past the lace curtains fastened back from the front window, he could see the lobby was neat, furnished with a tufted, blue sofa and two chairs with curled, wooden armrests. The pieces sat in neat order atop a colorful braided rug. Beyond was the tall desk where they would check in. It looked to be a respectable establishment. Of course…

He turned his head to look at the trussed up woman in boy's clothing beside him. Walking into a hotel lobby with a woman tethered on the end of a rope and a dog that was not, well, wasn't at all respectable. From the look on Penny's face, she was having the same thought.

After setting Frank on the ground, Garrett helped Penny down from her horse. Clearly, she was furious with him again, or still, because she kicked at him twice in the process. The first one missed, but her second effort landed the toe of her fancy boot against his hip.

"Stop that," he ordered, giving her a little shake.

"Then cut this rope, you, you savage."

"No," he said, and then, tugging on the rope, led her toward the steps of the hotel.

She dug her heels into the dirt and heaved back on the rope before shouting in a hushed voice, "You can't possibly walk me in there on a leash."

"Can I trust you to do as you're told?"

"I am not your servant!"

"No, you're my prisoner."

"Your...You said I was in protective custody. I've committed no crime."

"You just assaulted a U.S. Marshal."

"I did no such thing!"

"I'm going to have a bruise on my hip where you just kicked me."

She gasped. "I was defending myself. That doesn't count."

"It counts," he said, tugging on the rope again, hard enough to force her to trail along behind him. Her steps were loud as she stomped in protest up the wooden stairs. They entered the lobby of the hotel with her muttering something about dim-witted savages. The dog wagged his tail in broad swishes as he trotted along beside Garrett, apparently taking no offence to the way he'd bound Penny. Maybe Frank understood his reasoning better than Penny did. Garrett liked that dog more and more.

At the desk, a neat, narrow man with dark slicked back hair and a long nose greeted them.

"We need a room," Garrett told him.

"Two," Penny said.

"One," Garrett told the clerk. At her horrified look, he added, "One with a privacy screen." This didn't mollify her in the least. Her mouth hung open and her eyes sharpened in anger.

The man squinted at Penny, took in her unusual appearance, not hiding his surprise at the rope tied around her waist. He followed it to Garrett's hand.

Garrett opened his coat to show his badge.

"She's my prisoner," Garrett said.

"I most certainly am not!"

Without looking at her, he said to the man behind the desk, "She is."

The clerk leaned toward Garrett and whispered, "Is she dangerous?"

Penny gasped. "No, I'm not dangerous!"

"Don't worry," Garrett assured the clerk. "I'll keep her restrained."

Penny turned a glare on him so fierce he felt it all the way to his funny bone.

Tipping his head toward Frank, the clerk said, "We don't take dogs here, sir."

"The dog is an eye witness. He's in protective custody."

"Oh, I'm a prisoner, but the dog is in protective custody!" Penny yelled, her temper overrunning decorum.

"His name is Frank," Garrett said, flicking a glance toward Penny.

"I know his name," she bit out, looking like she wanted to bite Garrett. "I named him."

"She does have a temper, doesn't she?" the clerk said.

"That she does."

The clerk looked at Frank again. "Well, if the dog is in your protective custody, I suppose we could make an exception."

"You ask if I'm dangerous, but not the dog?" Penny asked, her outrage now directed at the clerk.

The clerk looked in askance to the marshal.

Garrett said, "The dog's not dangerous. He's a

victim." After a beat, Garrett added, "Too."

"Too?" Penny said, louder than necessary.

Garrett rubbed his hip, his expression overly pained.

Penny crossed her arms. "Oh, for goodness sakes."

The clerk stretched up on his toes and gave Frank a good once over. His eye paused at the bandage wrapped around the dog's hind leg.

"Oh, the poor thing," he said, and then inflicted Penny with a look of scathing disapproval. "I had a wonderfully loyal dog when I was a boy. I don't hold much with people who abuse animals."

"I did *not* abuse this dog! Garrett, tell him!"

"It's always the innocent looking ones you have to watch out for," Garrett said to the clerk, his face composed to utter seriousness.

Penny gasped again. The clerk gave a solemn nod.

Turning back to Garrett, the clerk said, "We have other guests. Are you sure you can keep her in check?"

"This is absurd. Garrett, I insist you tell him the truth, this instant. I'm completely serious."

Garrett had a hard time keeping a straight face when he said to the clerk, "I'll put extra restraints on her just to be safe."

From the corner of his eye, Garrett could see the blush of her embarrassment getting lost beneath the rising crimson of her rage.

"That'll be two dollars for the room," the clerk said.

"I'd also like two hip tubs sent up," Garrett told the clerk.

"That'll be fifty cents extra for a bath, each."

Garrett paid the man. "Our horses are right outside

with our saddlebags."

"I'll have your bags sent up so you won't have to leave your prisoner unguarded," the clerk said, slanting a fearful glance at Penny.

Garrett firmed his grip on the rope, because Penny looked as though she might actually jump the desk just to get her hands around the man's throat.

"I can also have your horses taken over to the livery for you," the clerk said.

"Thank you. That's a big help."

The clerk handed him a key and said in a conspiratorial tone, "I put you in a room at the end of the hall so you won't have any neighbors." He then flicked another quick glance toward the prisoner. "In case she should make a fuss."

Garrett nodded and said, "Good idea." He then proceeded to lead a fuming Penny up the stairs, Frank trotting behind, tail wagging.

The room was a decent size. One door, one window, a small table with two chairs sat between the window and a red brick fireplace with kindling and logs at the ready. The wood floor was clean and polished. A blue quilt covered the only bed.

After Garrett closed the door behind them, he turned around and received a swift kick in the leg.

"Ouch! What the hell's the matter with you?"

"Prisoner! Dangerous!"

Smiling through the pain, he said, "Well, you *have* kicked me twice since we've been here."

"You're lucky I don't have my Winchester, Garrett Kincaid. I most certainly would shoot you!"

"With your aim I'd be safe. No, don't you even think about kicking me again. I'll tie up your legs. Then

I'd have to cut off all your clothes to bathe you."

"Bathe me! You'll do no such thing!"

With a raised brow he said, "Then behave yourself."

Before she could respond, there was a knock at the door.

"Who is it," Garrett asked. His hand automatically on his gun.

"You ordered two baths?"

He opened the door and two young men entered, each carrying a hip tub with a rolled up rug inside on which they would set them. They both had the same mop of blond hair and similar roundish faces. The same blue eyes set in sun-reddened skin. One was taller and a bit heavier, his features more serious. Likely, they were brothers. One was about fifteen years old, the other, oh, thirteen or so.

"Hello, sir," the older of the boys said to Garrett. They set down their tubs and shook hands with the marshal. "I'm James and this here is my little brother Willie." While they were both sneaking peeks at Penny, the younger of the two had a much looser grasp on discretion.

"I'm Marshal Kincaid, and this is Miss Penelope Wills."

"Is she really dangerous?" the younger one asked. His gape-eyed expression bore equal and copious amounts of fear and fascination.

His big brother leaned over to give his shoulder a shove and shouted a whisper to him to stop staring.

"Yes, son," Garrett said to young Willie. "Don't get too close to her, boys," Garrett told them in all seriousness, resisting the urge to rub his sore shin.

"We never seen a lady outlaw before," Willie said, his words full of awe.

"Oh, for goodness sakes," Penny started. "I am not—"

"You can put one of those tubs right here," Garrett said. Then he pointed to the other side of the bed. "And put the other over there."

"We'll be bringing up the hot water right away," James told him.

"What did she do?" Willie whispered to Garrett. His big brother shot him a chiding look that Willie completely ignored.

Garrett said in a lowered tone, "I'm not at liberty to say, but I will tell you this, you don't want to tangle with her, boys." Then he shivered for effect.

"Oh, for goodness sakes," Penny mumbled, crossing her arms and turning her head away.

The boys exchanged a nervous glance before putting the tubs where Garrett had indicated, Willie carrying his to the far side of the room where he had to pass by Penny. On his way back, she gave him a sweet smile. Panic overtook his fascination, and the boy simultaneously picked up his step while whipping his face away from her.

"Is there anything else you'd like us to get for you, sir?" James said.

Garrett looked around the room again. "I don't see a privacy screen."

"We'll bring it up with your things," James told him. "And we'll take care of your horses, too."

"Appreciate it."

"I like your dog," Willie said when Frank approached the boy and nudged his hand for a pat. The boy was happy to oblige. "If you like, I could walk him for you."

"Thanks, that'd be nice."

"And if you like," said the older boy. "We could take your prisoner for a walk, too. If we each held a rope on opposite sides of her she wouldn't be able to get to either one of us."

"What! You most certainly will not *walk me,*" she declared.

Garrett nearly busted a gut holding back his laughter.

"And I'll tell you something else," Penny said, taking a crisp, angry step toward the boys.

The brothers jumped backward at the same time Garrett gave the rope a good yank. Penny lost her footing for a moment before her shoes found the floor again. With a grunt, her back slammed hard against his chest. She struggled to get away, but he held firm.

"See what I mean, boys," Garrett told them as Penny fought to escape him. "Dangerous."

"Come on, Willie," James said, tugging on his brother's sleeve. "Let's go get their things." The boys back-stepped out of the room, wide eyes stuck on Penny, and then turned to scamper down the hall as if they'd just faced the devil himself.

"You are not a gentleman," Penny snarled over her shoulder after the boys had gone.

"Never claimed to be." He gave her enough slack so she could step away from him, but he did not let go of the rope.

Beside herself with insult, Penny unleashed an angry tirade on him. "And you're a liar, and a bully, and a cad, and, and a liar!"

"You already said liar."

"It deserved repeating." Garrett didn't let her see him smile. He'd endured enough kicks for one day.

While waiting for their baths, Penny stomped from one end of the room to the other, as far from Garrett as her tether would allow. Twice she paused to glare at him and jerk at the rope. Though it was useless, it didn't stop her from doing it a third time.

The boys brought up plenty of hot water and set the privacy screen beside the tub on the far side of the room. Both the door and the window were on his side. Garrett wasn't worried about the window. Below it was only a narrow ledge, no trellis and the awning was several yards away to the right over the entrance to the hotel. If he wanted to get any sleep tonight, though, he'd have to do something about that door.

Even though the hip tub didn't allow them to stretch out, it did not detract from the enjoyment of a soak in clean, hot water. For a while, they were quiet, the only sound in the room was the gentle swirl and soft splash of bath water. Frank dozed in peace at the hearth.

The room dimmed, and Garrett looked toward the window to see the sun was nearing the end of its watch. The room had faded to burnished gold. Outside the air was chilled, but James had started a fine fire before leaving. Tonight they'd sleep in comfort and warmth.

Garrett turned toward the neatly made bed. He'd taken advantage of her once. He would not do it again, he vowed, no matter how much he wanted her. And he did want her. Penny was the most desirable woman he'd ever known, though it confounded him. She could be frustrating, and certainly infuriating. Garrett reminded himself she was also a proper lady, the day's events aside, and deserved to be treated so.

Glancing at the rope he tossed on the floor, he figured he was off to a bad start in that department. He couldn't leave her alone, for fear she'd run off and do something that could get her killed. Staying the night with her in this room, however, and not touching her, was going to be the most difficult thing he'd ever done in his life.

Penny deserved wooing, a proper proposal, and marriage to a stationary man. What could he offer her now? Marriage to a man who was never there? He traveled so much with his job he hardly saw his own family. If he took Penny to wife, he'd condemn her to a life of worry and loneliness.

Garrett turned his head toward the privacy screen. All he could see was a distorted image through the gauzy ripples of peach-colored fabric. Penny was there soaking in her tub, like a soft and flawless dream you can only almost touch.

Was she still mad? He wondered. Oh, yes. A grin touched his lips, but it was fleeting. Suddenly, he didn't want her mad at him. He wanted to see her smile. She wouldn't be smiling tomorrow, of course, when he had the sheriff keep her in a jail cell while he rode off after Zeke Cotter and Bentley Werner. She wouldn't understand he was trying to protect her. Tonight, though, they could have peace. They both deserved it.

"I'm sorry," Garrett said, breaking the silence.

Before responding, Penny turned to stare at the screen beside her tub. She sat still long enough for the last ripple of water to smooth. In all her life, she'd never been as angry with anybody as she was with Garrett Kincaid. She considered ignoring him, forever.

The man was high-handed and unreasonable, and had the manners of an ornery goat.

"For?" He had a lot to be sorry for and Penny wanted it verbalized. The man was an absolute wretch, dragging her through the lobby of a fine hotel on a leash! He'd treated Frank with more respect. How she ever found that man attractive was beyond her.

"For the way things turned out," he said.

"And?"

Garrett smiled as he inspected the spot where she'd kicked him. It was sore. He deserved it, though. His mother would have his hide if she knew how he'd treated a woman, especially one who wasn't actually a criminal.

"And for making you walk into the hotel at the end of a rope," he said.

"And?"

Garrett chuckled in a quiet breath that skimmed across the water. "And for telling everyone you were a dangerous outlaw."

Penny ran a drenched cloth down her throat, and then, taking her time, down both of her arms. The hot water had done much to calm her. The fact he was acknowledging his wrongdoing was also having a soothing effect. Penny had to remind herself that, at least in his mind, he was trying to keep her safe. She *had* caused him some worry in a dramatic fashion that probably would have had her own father seeking outrageous methods to see to her safety. Her fantasy of seeing Garrett thoroughly flogged now seemed a bit harsh.

Finally, she said, "I accept your apology."

"And?" Garrett said, unable to resist. He was

staring at the screen. He could only see her rippled shadow, growing murkier with the setting sun, but there was still light enough so he could see the slow revolution as she turned her head toward him. In his mind, Penny's cross expression was clear enough. Before she even spoke, he was smiling again.

"And what?" she asked, her tone indicating it better be good.

"And aren't you going to apologize for kicking me?"

"For…"

"Actually, you kicked me twice, but in the spirit of peace-seeking, one apology will suffice."

Water splashed from behind the screen. Her shadow twitched. She mumbled something in a harsh whisper he couldn't make out, but sounded to him like a sting of unladylike curses. He chuckled again, quietly, of course.

"Fine, I'm sorry I kicked you."

She didn't sound all that sorry, but the moment was all about forgiveness so he accepted her apology. Besides, while he enjoyed the banter, he needed to turn it serious. He didn't want Penny to worry about him taking advantage of the situation.

"I want to apologize for something else, too," Garrett said in all sincerity. "It's about what happened between us, last night."

It was the first time either of them had mentioned what they'd done beneath her blankets. She was hoping he'd just forget about it. Her shameless reaction to his touch and her declaration of love had left her entirely humiliated. He must think her a woman of no morals whatsoever. She'd be even more embarrassed if Garrett knew, even as angry as she'd been with him this day, how much she wanted to feel his touch once again.

"I acted in a wholly inappropriate manner," Garrett said. "And I'm sorry. It won't happen again."

He was apologizing? Those intimate moments he shared with her were about the only thing he'd done for which she felt he did not owe an apology. It was the one circumstance where he'd been kind and gentle. Garrett had given her pleasures she never knew existed. She couldn't admit she liked it, though, could she? Penny gnawed on her lower lip while trying to decide what she should say.

She was saying nothing, and her silence was making Garrett nervous. Maybe her anger was covering something else. The thought of her fearing him made him sick. But maybe she did, after what he'd done last night, after what Bentley almost did to her today.

"I won't touch you again, Penny. You have my word. You don't have to be afraid of me."

"I'm not afraid of you," she answered right away. She wanted to say more. She wanted to tell Garrett that his touch didn't frighten her, but made her feel more alive than she ever had in her life. But how to phrase it, and should she? Certainly, a lady didn't speak of such things. Penny's chin dipped and she stared at her hair floating in the water.

"Good. I'm glad to hear that." Garrett leaned back, thinking the matter settled, until another disturbing thought occurred to him. He sat up again and turned toward the screen. "Penny, I hope you're not feeling…you didn't do anything wrong. It was all me."

Penny used her finger to spin circles in her bath water, grateful for the screen between them. She could never discuss this with him if they were face to face. "After the way I behaved…"

"You behaved like a woman," he said, sitting up straighter before leaning over the tub. You've nothing to be ashamed of, Penny, nothing at all."

He was defending her. While that pleased her immensely, she was intrigued with the information he was willing to impart. She wanted to know more. Her curiosity was piqued, and the screen between them emboldened her.

"That…that was normal?" Penny asked.

Leaning back, Garrett kept his eyes on the murky shadow behind the screen. It occurred to him that since her mother died when she was quite young, and she didn't have any other female relatives, no one had ever explained things to her. His actions certainly didn't help matters any. Last night, he'd probably left her confused by her own feelings.

Garrett sighed and ran a wet hand down his face, barely noticing the smoothness of his fresh shave. It wasn't his place to have this talk with her, but since he'd been the one to introduce her to that world, it was now his obligation.

"That's part of what happens between a man and a woman," he told her. "Yes, it's perfectly normal."

"So…you don't think poorly of me?"

There was a thread of concern in her voice and it shamed him. Turning his body toward the screen fast enough to slosh water over the edge of the tub, he said, "Is that what you think? No, I don't think poorly of you, not at all. Seeing you like that, well." He sat back again, his body remembering the need she stirred as much as his mind. Just thinking about it roused him

155

again. "Penny, it was the most beautiful thing I've ever known."

Garrett turned his head to stare at the screen, wishing badly he could see her face, to hold her and reassure her. He wanted something else, too. In this odd moment of simultaneous privacy and intimacy, he was able to admit he wanted to hear her say she loved him again. He wanted to hear it not in the throes of passion, not in her confusion of feelings, and not just once more. He wanted to hear it every day for the rest of his life. The realization jarred him, and it drew from him a yearning that pressed through every pore, nearly hauling him from the tub in a powerful desire to get to her.

But no, it couldn't be. Garrett turned away from the screen, away from the only woman who had ever gotten under his skin. His initial reasonings had been right. He could not sentence her to a life she would have to live virtually alone, watching out the window, wondering every day when her husband would return to spend but a few days with her before leaving again to chase outlaws, wondering if this time he would come back at all. He could give her children, sure, but she'd be there to raise them by herself most of the time. Penny deserved better.

Garrett closed his eyes against a pain more searing than the graze of a bullet, sharper than the finely honed blade of a knife.

Penny's fingers grasped the edge of the tub. "Garrett…about what I said to you last night."

He shifted in a slow turn to gaze at her silhouette, gripping the rim of his tub, dreading the words, and yet willing them to come. If she said them, he would say it back this time because he did love her. He wanted her love, her body, the rest of her life, all for himself, wanted to haul her in front of a preacher this very minute and claim her all right and legal for the whole world to know. But if he gave up his career, what would he do?

He was a U.S. Marshal. Being a lawman wasn't just his job, it's who he was right down to his marrow. He couldn't go back to farming. He wasn't a farmer anymore. He'd have to be, though, if he wanted to support a family without leaving them alone for weeks, even months at a time.

Staring at her silhouette behind the screen, Garrett knew he would sacrifice his career in law for her. He would pay any price if in this moment of utter clarity he could hear her say those three words again.

Penny glanced at the screen beside her tub. He was so quiet. Was he worried she would tell him she loved him again? Was he afraid she'd gone marriage minded and was trying to corner him? The fact that she did love him both irritated and pleased her. It also terrified her. He didn't feel the same way about her, obviously. She was a naïve little fool and Garrett was simply trying to spare her feelings.

"About what I said…"

"Yes?" Garrett prompted when she didn't continue. Why didn't he just say it first? Garrett knew the answer before he'd finished the question. He didn't want her to doubt those words, and she might. The room had one bed. It wasn't unheard of for a man to use those precious words to get a woman between the sheets. If Penny said it first, though, he could lay his heart bare for her. And he would. If he had to bust sod the rest of his days, he'd do it, if it meant he could spend those days with Penny.

The silence in the room intensified. In the hearth, the flames barely shimmied. Even the daylight slanting through the window held still, as if pausing in its descent.

"I…"

Garrett and Penny both sat in similar deportment, facing each other on opposite sides of the gauzy privacy screen.

Penny bit her lip to keep from blurting out her feelings hadn't changed, that she did love him. He was bossy and arrogant, but he was also heroic. Garrett was a man of honor. He took his job seriously and she'd spent the last two days making his job more difficult. If she told him what was in her heart, it would only make things worse for him. He didn't share her feelings. He certainly would have said so by now if he did.

"I'm sorry about that, too," Penny said, just loud enough for him to hear.

Garrett sat back in the cooling water. After a moment, he mumbled. "No need to apologize." It was better this way, he reminded himself. He was good at his job and there was important work that needed doing. The inner discourse didn't make him feel better, though. In fact, he felt like hell.

After the boys had collected the water and hauled away the tubs, Garrett tied the rope he'd used on Penny around Frank's neck so James and Willie could take him for a walk.

"We'll give him a bath, too," Willie said.

"For an extra charge, of course," added his big brother.

"I wouldn't expect you to work for free, boys. A bath is a fine idea." Stepping out into the hall with the boys, Garrett gave them another errand to run, too.

He and Penny ate a quiet dinner in their room at the small table between the fireplace and the window. The scene was cozy, lovely, really, after the last days they had spent out on the road. They were warm and clean, yet wound tight with the unresolved tension of their true desires.

Around the time they were down to just picking at what was left of their dinners, the boys returned with Frank. The dog was clean, still a little damp, in fact. Garrett rubbed the dog's head and caught a whiff of something more pleasant than wet dog. He bent down to give Frank a sniff.

"We sprinkled some of our ma's rose water on him," Willie told him.

Garrett smiled, sure their mother was unaware her boys had used her rose water to freshen up a dog. "He smells good, like a flower garden."

"We fed him, too," Willie added.

Garrett turned to James then who stuffed his hand into his pocket and pulled out three silver bells tied together with several long, sturdy strings. He handed the mess to the marshal who thanked them and gave them both a generous tip before sending them on their way.

"What's that for?" Penny asked after he closed the door.

Garrett tied the string of bells onto the doorknob. "It's so you don't go sneaking out of here in the middle of the night."

Penny didn't argue. He didn't know if it was

159

because she surrendered to his command or because she believed she could sneak past the bells. Right now, she was preoccupied with other thoughts, he could see, as she was looking at the bed.

Garrett took the blanket folded at the foot of the bed, scooted Frank out of the way and laid it on the rug before the fire. Then he took one of the pillows and tossed it on the blanket.

"You're sleeping on the floor?" she asked.

"Unless you want to share the bed with me," Garrett said, his voice more gruff than he'd intended.

"No, of course not," she replied. Penny used the best of her learned propriety to shield her pride. No matter what he said, after the way she'd behaved last night, he might be under the impression she wanted to share the bed with him. It aggravated her that he'd be right.

"Go to sleep, Penny."

Penny spun away from him in a swirl of wrinkled, white cotton, and slipped beneath the covers. She scooted to the far side and lay with her back to Garrett. A moment later, Frank hopped up on the bed and walked in a circle before lying down beside Penny. Garrett looked at Frank who returned his gaze with one tinged with regret. Not too much regret, though. The wry notion picked at him as the dog made himself comfortable on the soft mattress.

Garrett lay down with his blanket beside the dwindling fire. With his head pillowed in his hands, he stared at the ceiling. At a rustling from the bed, he turned to look, thinking that maybe Penny would be peeking over the edge at him, wondering if she was thinking about him the way he was thinking about her.

No, that would be impossible. She didn't have the experience to put those explicit images in her head.

Instead of an inviting look from Penny, he got an eyeful of Frank's furry snout poking over the edge of the bed. The dog snuffled once. Maybe it was a condolence. Maybe the raggedy beast was gloating.

Watch her, Garrett mouthed to the dog with a nod toward Penny.

Frank puffed air from his nostrils, which Garrett took as a 'yes sir'. The dog then disappeared again. The mattress springs creaked as Frank settled into the cozy bed, followed by a contented sigh as Frank drifted off for a good night's sleep. The damn dog was having a better life than Garrett was. The scene was so ridiculous, him on the floor while a dog lay in the bed next to Penny, he could almost laugh about it. Almost.

He sure as hell wasn't laughing when he woke up the next day. Penny was gone, again.

Chapter 10

"Penny!" Garrett shouted as he sat up on the floor where he'd slept. He looked toward the privacy screen standing across the room, lifeless, as no shadow moved behind it.

He called out her name even though his gut told him he was talking to no one. Oddly, he'd sensed her absence the second the morning sunshine thrust through the window and landed on his face. He knew she was gone before he even opened his eyes.

"Penelope Wills!" he yelled, jumping to his feet.

Frank jerked into a sitting position atop the otherwise empty bed, looking sleepy and rankled. Garrett ignored him. He stomped across the room, grabbed the screen, and flung it to the floor. Frank barked once. Garrett gave him a quelling look. The dog put his ears back, managing to appear both offended and apologetic.

Garrett stomped over to the door. The bells were in place. He flicked the sting with his finger and they all three rang out, just as he had planned. Then, with a sickening fear, Garrett turned in a slow rotation toward the window.

It was open. When they'd gone to sleep last night, he knew he'd left it closed.

He ran to the window and shoved his head out through the full opening. Garrett looked down hoping his memory of the narrow ledge was incorrect. But no, he remembered it right. The ledge was no more than a foot wide. His stomach roiled at his mind's image of her inching her way along toward the awning off to the right, and then climbing down the pole. This of course, is exactly what she'd done.

Damn her!

He scanned the street below…pointless. Penny was long gone.

Garrett pulled his head in and looked to the corner where he'd placed her Winchester. It was still there. His gun was still there, too, lying on the floor next to his bedding. He grabbed his bag. The gun Penny had taken from Bentley was gone.

"Damn it all to hell!" he shouted. He swore several more times, and several degrees more vulgar in the few seconds it took him to kick his feet into his boots. He was out the door before his body heat had evaporated from the blanket, Frank at his heels.

Garrett questioned the clerk, the same prim man who'd been there when they'd checked in. Worry wrinkling his smooth forehead, he told the marshal he hadn't seen his prisoner.

"You promised you could keep her restrained," the clerk said in an accusatory panic, but Garrett was already halfway to the door.

He ran past the restaurant attached to the hotel by way of an open arch, giving it only a cursory glance. Penny hadn't snuck out of a second story window to go have breakfast. She was going after Cotter.

Garrett burst onto the boardwalk and then stopped to think. Frank took the opportunity to relieve himself on the very pole Penny shimmied down sometime last night, damn her. The day was bright with a potential to warm, not that he noted the weather. Garrett focused all of his attention on finding that blasted woman who seemed determined to worry him into an early grave.

The day was just beginning and only a few people were about. Across the street was a dress shop. A slender woman in a pine-green gown with a matching, thin brimmed hat was unlocking the door. Several other businesses were beginning to open, too. Next to the dress shop, a young man emerged from the milliner's with a broom in his hand. Just inside the window beside the door, a woman rearranged a display of bonnets.

Two dusty cowboys passed by on their horses, apparently in no hurry. A Conestoga wagon ambled in from the other direction. From inside the covered wagon he could hear the voices of several children singing. There was no sign of Penny.

The outside door to the restaurant was to the right and a shop not yet opened was to the left. Next to that was a saloon. A sign over the boardwalk dangling from two short chains read, The Rusty Nail. All was quiet in both directions. Garrett turned to his right and ran for the stables.

Almost as soon as he entered the stables, he found Penny's speckled mare. The horse was nibbling on some sweet hay. Lady Bell was right beside Lulu. Good, Penny was on foot. That'll make it easier. Now, where would she start? She was an inexperienced investigator, but not stupid. Well, with the exception of her personal safety, he amended with an audible growl. Garrett and Frank ran back to the saloon. He had the dog wait outside, hoping he'd bark if he saw Penny.

The gaming tables inside The Rusty Nail were

empty, the winners, and losers asleep in their beds. The other tables were empty, too. The place had a well-worn look about it, but it was roomy. Lots of scarred tables, the green cloths over the faro and poker tables had faded in the places where they got the most play, the gold fringe on one table hung loose. There was an upright piano against the far wall. The round stool before it sat empty.

The two cowboys he'd seen ride in sat at end of the bar. They glanced at him, and then turned their attention back to their breakfasts of whiskey. Garrett approached the bartender who barely looked up from the glass he was cleaning.

"Name's Smoky," he said with a pleasant smile his profession required. "What can I get you?

He was a barrel of a man with arms like tree trunks and a nose crooked enough to tell it had been broken, at least once. His dust-colored hair was thinning and frizzed above leathery skin. However, the graying didn't deter from his tough presentation in the least. Smoky here had broken up his share of bar fights and left the troublemakers to regret crossing him. In one meaty hand, he held a glass, in the other, a rag with which he was wiping it dry. Scrapes marred both sets of his knuckles.

"Has a young woman been in here today, about so tall?" He held his hand chin high. "Blonde, pretty, dressed in boy's clothing and asking questions."

Smokey was nodding before Garrett finished his description. "She was in here all right," he said on a chuckle. "Behaving all proper, just like she was wearin' a ball gown, she was. Even dressed like that, she was a pretty thing, friendly too, but serious. Said she was working with a U.S. Marshal on a federal matter, a manhunt. That be you?"

Pressed for time, Garrett merely grunted a non-response. "Do you know where she went from here?"

"She was looking for someone. Don't remember the name, but she had a good description of him. A fella looked just like that was in here last night."

Garrett stiffened. "Tell me about him."

"Well, the man looked a rough sort with a bad scar on his face, and he didn't smell too good, neither. But he was quiet, didn't bother no one. Had himself a few drinks 'fore he took himself upstairs with one of our girls, Slena. Musta fallen asleep, and I guess Slena let him be. He left here not more than an hour ago."

"Do you know where he went from here?"

Smokey frowned at him. "I don't pry into my customers' personal business."

"Where's Slena now?"

Smokey tipped his jaw toward the upstairs. "She's up there, room three. Your girl went up and talked to her, left about twenty minutes ago."

Garrett took the stairs two at a time.

The young woman who answered the door was not sleepy-eyed and annoyed, as he'd expected. In fact, she was wide-awake and dressed in a surprisingly simple calico buttoned all the way to her throat. She had light brown hair wrapped into a tidy bun on the back of her head. Pale yellow ribbons dangled from the bonnet she held in her hand. The woman looked more like a Sunday school teacher than a prostitute. Her modest and alert appearance threw Garrett off for a moment.

"Slena?" he asked.

She lifted the chin of her freshly washed face.

"Selina. The proper way to say my name is Selina. And I'm not open for business, ever again."

"I'm not here for…that. I'm looking for a young woman named Penelope Wills. You might know her as Penny."

Her expression immediately brightened. Selina's eyes slid to the badge pinned to his shirtfront. "She told me she had a partner in the investigation. You must be Penny's associate."

"Her…" Garrett held his tongue. He didn't have time to set her right and he had a feeling Penny had so won the girl over that speaking of her with anything less than praise would get the door slammed in his face.

"Yes," he said through a forced smile. "That's right. I just have a couple of questions."

Selina opened her door further and said, "All right. You can talk while I finish packing."

He entered the small room, the contents of which consisted of one narrow bed, an old bureau with a round mirror over it, and a little closet. An old carpetbag sat upon the neatly made bed. It was open and she'd already begun packing her belongings. On the only chair in the room was a pile of bright and bawdy clothing.

"Here, sit down," she said, scooping up the pile from the chair and moving it to the bed. "I'm not taking these things with me. Figured I'd leave them for the next girl."

Garrett stood where he was. "You're quitting the business?"

"Your partner convinced me. She said I'm a worthy person, and I deserved better than this kind of life. And you know what, she's right," Selina said with

167

a firm nod of her head.

Garrett couldn't help but smile. He had no trouble at all imagining Penny riling this girl into betterment. If she'd spent much more time here, Smokey would have to close the upstairs portion of his business.

"I had a little money saved and that sweet angel gave me the rest of the money I needed to buy a ticket on the next stage out of here. I have folks in Nebraska." Selina smiled, then, looking happy enough to weep. "I'm going home."

She continued to sing Penny's praises while she packed the rest of her few belongings into the bag and then closed and latched it. She started to lift it off the bed, but Garrett got it for her.

"Thanks," Selina said. "The morning stage is leaving soon. I don't want to miss it."

As they left her room, Garrett said, "Did Penny happen to say where she was going from here?"

"After that man I had up here last night. Didn't she tell you?"

"We keep missing each other," he said, following her down the stairs.

"Oh, well, like I told your partner, the man with the big scar on his face asked me where he could get a decent breakfast. I told him the hotel served breakfast, but he said that was too fancy for his taste. So, I told him about Dixie's. She opens a little earlier anyway. Her place is two blocks past the hotel; make a left and one block up."

As they neared the bottom of the stairs, Garrett looked to his left. The two cowboys were gone, and the bartender was nowhere in sight, for which he was grateful. The last thing he needed right now was to get held up helping Selina out of an ugly scene.

He'd sprung his gratitude a bit too soon.

Just then, the curtain hanging over the doorway behind the bar flapped and Smokey emerged. He took one look at Selina and the bag in Garrett's hand, and said to Selina, "Where the hell do you think you're going?"

Selina squared her shoulders. "I quit, Smoky."

"You can't quit on me now," he said, incredulous. "I'm already a couple girls short."

"I'm sorry about that, but I have to do what's best for me."

Smokey's demeanor turned dark. Anger deepened the color of his bronzed skin. His back even hunched a little. He turned a furious gaze on Garrett.

"You convince her to leave her job here?"

"Me? No. I'm just carrying her bag for her."

Smoky stomped out from behind the bar and right up to Garrett. "She was just fine with things until you went up there."

"I didn't turn her mind. Anyway, it's a free country. If the girl wants to leave, she can leave."

"I knew it! You takin' her to St. Louis, one of those fancy places to work for you? What did you promise her, more money, better conditions, what?"

"Calm down, Smoky. The girl's not going away with me," Garrett said, bending to set down the bag. He was trying to placate the man before things got out of hand. He soon found out just how miserably he failed. When he stood upright, a hard fist to the face was there to meet him.

Selina screamed, Garrett heard. He couldn't see what was happening because he was flat on his back facing the cobwebs in the ceiling and marveling at how quickly the skin on his cheekbone grew tight from swelling. It occurred to him this was the second time he'd found himself in this position since he'd met Miss Penelope Wills.

Then he heard Smoky utter a grunt, and the floor beneath him vibrated with a very heavy thud. Garrett hauled himself up on his elbows. Smoky lay curled up on his side, gasping for breath, whimpering, both hands clutching his manhood. Garrett looked up at Selina, who proudly smiled down on him.

"I have to go now," she said, straightening out her skirts. "I don't want to miss the stage."

Garrett swiveled his head again to look at Smoky, and even though the bastard had surely given him a black eye, he felt for the guy. That was some mighty suffering she'd put upon him. He turned his astonished gaze back to Selina.

"It's kind of funny, you know?"

"What's that?" Garrett asked, seeing nothing funny at all about the situation. He'd come in for information on a woman who'd done what no man ever had, escaped him, twice. Following that was something else that had never happened to him before; he lost a fight without getting in a single lick. Now he was lying on the dirty floor of a saloon with a blackening eye after a recently retired prostitute had to come to his rescue. No, nothing was funny at all.

"Smoky is the one who taught me that move, you know, how to take down a man. He said it was in case any of the customers ever got too rough with me. I never had to use it before today. It really works."

In Garrett's opinion, she looked way too happy

with her success in de-manning her employer. Smoky whimpered on the floor beside him. Yeah, it worked all right.

Garrett got to his feet and picked up Selina's bag. They left Smoky moaning on the floor. Nothing they could do for the poor man. They pushed through the doors to the saloon and onto the boardwalk, where Frank sat waiting. Ten minutes later, Selina was waving goodbye from the window of the stage. Garrett turned and headed for Dixie's.

The restaurant was full of chattering people and bursting with the smell of coffee and grease. He took a quick but thorough look around. Neither Penny nor Cotter was in the restaurant. In the center of the room stood a rather large, matronly woman with strong hands and iron gray hair twisted into a tight knot atop her head. The aproned woman set down a couple of loaded plates at a table where two men eagerly awaited their meals. He got to her as she was turning around.

"Excuse me," he said loud enough so she could hear him over the mixed conversations and the clattering of dishes and silverware. "Are you Dixie?"

"That's me," she said, in a voice accustomed to speaking up loud. "Just find a seat. I'll be right with you."

"I'm not here to eat." Tapping a finger on his badge, he said, "I'm looking for a couple of people." He quickly described Penny and Cotter. She nodded as her face pinched in aggravation. "Oh boy," Garrett muttered to himself, wondering what Penny had done now.

"They were here all right," Dixie said, a frown stitching her thick eyebrows together as she crossed her arms over an ample bosom. "She came in not too long after he did. She sat across the restaurant to his back where he couldn't see her. I saw her watching him while he ate. When I went to take her order, she said she didn't want anything. I told her if she was going to take up one of my tables she had to order something, so she asked for hotcakes. She didn't eat a single bite, though. The girl never took her eyes off that man. Then, he happened to turn around and he saw her. Appeared to recognize her, too."

"What happened then?" Garrett asked, his chest tightening.

"I'll tell you what happened," she said with a sharp nod as her hands moved to clasp the bulges of her hips.

"He ran out of the restaurant without paying for his meal, that's what happened. And then you know what? That girl jumped up and ran right out after him, without paying for hers, either."

"Did you see which way they went?"

Dixie crossed her arms in front of her again, steel bands locking away his information. "Did I mention they didn't pay for their meals?"

Garrett scowled at her.

"They left owing for their breakfasts. That's fifteen cents, each."

"Are you trying to blackmail a federal officer?" He crossed his arms, too, just under his badge. Dixie was not impressed.

"Worry over the loss of income does seem to affect my memory."

Since he didn't have time to argue or make threats he'd then have to carry through, Garrett paid the debt. He'd take it out of Penny's hide once he caught up with her.

The woman dropped the coins into her apron pocket with one hand and waved her other toward the door. "He made a left when he ran out of here. I saw through the window. Your girl followed, both of them at a full run."

"Do you know where he was going?"

"How should I know? I gotta get back to work now." She turned away, but he stepped in front of her to block her way. He was going to get his thirty cents worth of information.

"Did the man say anything to you earlier, anything that might tell me where he might have gone?"

She huffed out an angry breath, but then said, "After I took his order, he asked where the telegraph office was. That was the direction he was headed when he bolted."

"The tele…"

"Dixie!"

At the shout from the kitchen, she turned her back on Garrett and left without another word.

Garrett made a left out of Dixie's, and he and Frank moved at a brisk pace past the feed store, wondering why Cotter would be looking for the telegraph office. It couldn't be Bentley. If Cotter sent or received a telegraph to or from Bentley Werner, others would know about it. At the very least, the telegraph operator would know, and that would connect the two men. Cotter might not be smart enough to figure in that mistake, but Bentley was.

Garrett ran by a blacksmith who was hard at work pounding a heavy mallet against red glowing metal and sending sparks flying. At the end of the street and around the corner to the left, he found the telegraph office. Garrett almost ran down an elderly man who was coming out the door.

"Slow down, son."

"Sorry," Garrett said as he steadied the old guy.

"You keep running through life like that, you'll miss all the good stuff." The old man gave him a friendly nod and shuffled on his way.

Garrett put one hand on his gun and with ingrained caution, opened the door with the other.

The telegraph office was empty, except for the young operator. He was skinny as a rail wearing thick spectacles, hunched near the window reading a book that appeared to weigh almost as much as he did. He looked up when Garrett walked in, stood up, and removed his spectacles.

"Mornin' sir. What can I do for you?"

Garrett identified himself, said he was looking for two people, and described both Penny and Zeke Cotter.

"Sorry, sir, the only one who's been in here today is old Mr. Findlay. He just left."

"Has a telegram come in for Zeke Cotter, maybe even yesterday or the day before?"

The clerk looked through some papers in a box beside his machine. "No, sir, nothing."

Flummoxed, Garrett nodded and said a quick thank you before stepping out of the telegraph office. He stood on the board walkway, thinking. It was entirely possible Bentley had instructed Cotter to expect a message in code. Using an alias, he could send any kind of simple telegram that wouldn't put suspicion on either man, yet meant it was time to meet.

It still didn't make sense. Why bother with a

telegram if they'd already arranged a meeting? Could be they had a place to meet, but the time had not been set. That would make sense. It was also possible Bentley never sent his message. After all, his plan had certainly gone awry. Garrett thought on it some more.

Cotter was an able-bodied man, big, but with legs considerably longer than Penny's. Surely, he could outrun her, lose her, and make his way back to the telegraph office. At least that's all he hoped Cotter would do.

As much as it killed him to do nothing but wait while both Penny and Cotter were out there gunning for each other, the fact was, Cotter had specifically asked where the telegraph office was. Garrett could run all over town looking for them, missing them, or he could wait in the one place Cotter was sure to come.

Garrett turned to take stock of his surroundings. On the boardwalk along the wall were two barrels and a chair. He moved the chair to position it between the barrels. He sat himself in the chair, leaned back, and tipped his hat forward until it was low on his brow. Frank was restless too, only the dog had the luxury of letting it show, moving all around him, sniffing furiously, as if he'd caught a scent.

The dog continued his hectic pace, his nose to the ground. Garrett ignored him and waited. He hated waiting.

Chapter 11

Penny emerged from her blackness, sluggish as molasses on a cold winter's morn. Her head hurt like the devil and for several minutes, disorientation had her thoughts scattered far and away. Then it all rushed back.

She could feel sticky warm blood between her hatless head and the dirt floor on which she lay. With her first attempt at movement, she found she was utterly helpless. A cloth tied at the back of her head covered her mouth and rough rope bound her ankles together and her hands behind her back. She didn't have to open her eyes to know where she was. Zeke Cotter held her captive in the small shack across the street and up the hill from the telegraph office.

She'd followed him here. He thought he'd outrun her, but she wasn't only fast wearing trousers instead of her skirts, she was sly, too. Just around the corner of a long stretch of the chase that had taken them around an entire block, she'd hidden, either in a doorway or between buildings so when he looked back he would think he'd lost her. And that's exactly what happened.

The arrogant outlaw slowed to a brisk walk, and with a lot of ducking and hiding, she'd followed him to the telegraph office. He looked at the sign for a moment, seemed satisfied he found what he had been looking for, but he didn't go inside. In fact, he turned his back to the shop and walked directly across the street and up the hill. When he walked around to the back of the small, wooden structure, Penny waited for a few minutes before she followed.

She'd pressed her ear against the shack,but heard nothing. Walking on the tips of her toes, she'd made her way around to the other side. She must not have been as sneaky as she'd thought, because Zeke Cotter was standing there, ready for her. Before she could point her gun, his rough hands lifted her by her collar, and he dragged her around the corner. He then slammed her against the shack a couple of times, hard enough to dislodge her hat. She'd caught a brief glimpse of his fist before the world turned black.

"I know yer awake," he said in a voice that sounded full of trail dirt. His pungent odor filled the room. Hard dirt crunched beneath his boots as he stepped closer. The sole of one of those boots then shoved into her ribs. "Open yer eyes."

She'd wanted more time to think first, but there was no hope for that now. Reluctantly, Penny opened her eyes to the dim and dusty room. She worked herself into a seated position, ignored the pounding in her head as well as the wave of nausea, and looked up into the face of the man who'd murdered her father.

With cruel slowness, Cotter slid his knife from the sheath at his waist and crouched down before her. He held it just inches in front of her face so she could get a good look at the big blade, surprisingly shiny and clean, and honed viciously sharp.

Penny felt dizzy at the sight but managed to stay upright. Cotter turned the knife until the blade caught a strip of sunlight slicing through one of the gaps in the boards. He paused there for an interminable moment. Once satisfied with her level of fear, the outlaw floated the knife until it touched the skin just above her shirt collar.

"If you scream," he said in a low, raspy voice, his fetid breath tacky across her face. "I'll slit your throat. You'll be dead before anyone gets here. Understand?"

All too aware of the placement of his knife, Penny gave only a very slight nod. Cotter then used his free hand to yank down the gag. His rancid odor lodged in her throat along with her fear and nearly choked her. She forced herself to focus, knowing that panic meant her death. The task was next to impossible with a killer before her, his cold blade resting against her throat.

"Marshal Kincaid will catch you," she said as soon as he leaned back, taking his knife with him. "You'll never get away with this."

The grin that split his scarred face was smug and made a show of his tobacco-stained teeth. He cleared his throat and spat into the corner of the small room. Penny turned away from him in disgust.

"He'll have to catch me first," Cotter said. Penny turned back to face him. He was still grinning. "Soon I'll have plenty of money to git me far, far away from here."

Cotter stood up and leaned his back against the wall, cleaning his filthy fingernails with the shiny tip of his knife. Clearly, he had no care for hygiene. He was just trying to frighten her. It was working.

Penny looked around the small shack. There were gaps in plenty of the boards that let enough sunlight in so she could see the room was empty, but for the two of them. Her hat sat on the ground a few feet away. She looked again for something she could use as a weapon. All there was to see were thick masses of dust motes pasted in strips of dull, yellow light. Not that it mattered. Even if there were something nearby she could use, the rough rope binding her hands had no give.

After a moment, Cotter held the knife before his face, turning it one way, and then the other, admiring his weapon. He moved it over until the well-tended blade caught in the sunlight again. His head tilted to the side as thoughts made a play across his marred face.

"You know," Cotter said, staring at his knife as if in a trance. "We got lots of time still. And I always kinda thought it would be fun to have someone all to myself like this."

Slowly, his eyes shifted from the long blade to land on Penny again, and her blood ran cold. Within those merciless depths, lurked a myriad of depravity. She twisted in the ropes binding her hands behind her back, her fingers rubbed raw at her frantic plucking.

Zeke Cotter grinned a little, just a little. The movement was small, but bursting with malevolence. "It's no use, purty girl. I'm real good at tyin'."

"The marshal is looking for me," Penny said, unable to keep the quiver from her voice.

After staring at Penny for an eternal moment, he took a step and crouched before her again. He slid the knife back into its sheath, and Penny dared to hope he just meant to frighten her from testifying against him.

He looked hard into her face, with that trance-like gaze again. Then he lifted the gag back over her mouth.

Zeke Cotter stared at her as if she were a struggling bug he was about to enjoy crushing. He slid out his knife and began circling it around her face. Penny turned away from him, but he pinched her jaw hard and jerked her forward again.

"By the time I get done with you, that marshal won't even recognize yer face."

Penny's mind worked at a furious pace. She could barely move. Nobody knew where she was. It would likely be a long while before anyone even found her here.

Cotter ran the knife down her shirtfront in a manner made more frightening by his gentle touch. The blade made a long, slow whisper against cloth, as if in the planning stage of a long list of things he wanted to do. Taking his time, enjoying himself, he slid the flat of the knife down one leg, and up the other. Penny scooted away from him until her back was against the boards. Cotter laughed. He held the knife straight up then, pointed at the ceiling. As if to take certain aim, he lowered his arm until the tip of the blade pointed at Penny's chest.

On his knees and with his free arm, he began crawling toward her, twirling the knife in a circle, enjoying his game.

He touched the tip of the blade to the hollow at the base of her throat. Penny pressed her head back against the board wall as far as she could. There was no doubt in her mind she was about to die. It wouldn't be quick, nor would it be painless. Her mind turned to Garrett and in the midst of her terror, worried he would blame himself for this.

She wanted to tell him she was sorry for causing him so much trouble.

She wanted to know his kiss again.

Penny thought of his arms around her and drew courage from the memory so she could die bravely. Tears filled her eyes as the point of the knife pierced her skin.

Then, for the second time in as many days, Frank came to her rescue.

At a furious scratching against the wall, Zeke Cotter swung his knife around. They both jumped at the sound of a loud bark. Another bark followed, and then another, the barks growing more frantic.

"What the hell is a dog doing here?" Cotter muttered before jumping to his feet. He sheathed his knife and drew his gun.

Penny made a frantic protest through the gag, but Cotter ignored her. With a slow movement, he turned the knob, and then in a burst, he shoved the door open and stepped outside. Sunlight poured in, blinding Penny. Frank gave out a long string of barks. A dull thud followed, and then Frank was silent. Penny closed her eyes, and the tears gathered for her hero dog.

But then, Frank was licking her face. Penny opened her eyes to find his furry snout and sparkling brown eyes. Working her mouth and using her shoulder, Penny was able to lower the gag.

"Frank, you overpowered him!"

"No," Garrett said from the door. "I did."

Chapter 12

Garrett stood, frozen in the doorway as if an arctic wind had blown through and turned him to solid ice. Seeing Penny like that, face swollen, head bloodied, a thin line of blood trickling from a cut at the base of her throat, he wanted to go out and pound the unconscious Zeke Cotter until the outlaw's ability to recover was long past.

"Garrett," Penny said. Tears filled her eyes until they flowed over the edge and down her face.

Her reaction to him set Garrett into motion. He untied her hands and feet, then took a cloth from his shirt pocket and used it to wipe the blood from her throat. The cut barely broke the skin, thank goodness. He then inspected the injury to her head. It was no longer bleeding, but it needed tending.

"Are you hurt anywhere else?" he asked, shocked at how difficult it was to get the words past the tightness in his throat.

"No," Penny answered, and then looked at his swollen eye. "What happened to your face?"

"Oh, that. It was a gift from your pal Smokey."

"That sweet man from the Rusty Nail? Whatever did you do to provoke him?"

"What did *I* do?"

"Does it hurt?" she asked, with a gentle touch to his face.

"I'm fine." *Now*. He lifted Penny to her feet and wrapped his arms around her. He buried his face in the soft curve of her neck. Her pulse beat against his cheek, and Garrett was sure nothing in his life had ever felt so good, not even close.

He understood now why he so wanted to hear her say again that she loved him. It was because he loved her, too, loved her the way his father had loved his mother. He loved her and he wasn't ever going to let her out of his sight again. If that meant tying bells to her feet every night, then that's what he would do.

"How did you find me?" she asked. She didn't loosen her hold. Neither did Garrett.

Frank rubbed himself against Garrett's leg, and Garrett glanced down while keeping Penny within the tight circle of his arms. His spill of emotions ran down to the dog. If it hadn't been for Frank's good nose and stubborn perseverance, things would have turned out quite different.

While he'd been sitting in front of the telegraph office waiting for Cotter to show up, Frank kept his nose to the ground. Then the dog moved into the road. The many mixed scents he found there threw him for a minute or so, but then he picked up the trail again. The dog was halfway up the hill toward the little wooden shack when he turned and ran back to the middle of the road, spinning in agitation and barking until Garrett caught on. All his years of experience had nothing on Frank's nose.

"Actually," Garrett admitted. "It was that dog. He followed your trail. I just followed him."

Penny twisted away then, and crouched down to hug the dog. "Oh, Frank. You're such a good dog!"

Frank accepted her hug and her praise, looking over her shoulder to give Garrett another one of those arrogant dog grins. This time, Garrett didn't mind. The dog had earned the right. Penny stood up and tipped her head back to look into Garrett's eyes.

They both spoke at the same time.

"Garrett."

"Penny."

At Garrett's nod to continue, she said, "I'm sorry for causing you worry."

"I have a feeling you're going to cause me all kinds of trouble over the next few decades."

"Decades? What are you talking about?"

He drew her back into his arms and leaned down to kiss her then, long and hard, possessing her mouth, as he would soon have the rest of her. She raised her arms to wrap them around his neck and kissed him back with equal fervor.

Finally, Garrett broke the kiss. He gazed down at her flushed face, at her kiss-swollen lips, at the dreamy lust in her eyes he knew couldn't possibly equal his, and said, "What I mean is we're getting married."

Penny stared at him for a moment, before blinking herself into coherency. "Married?"

Garrett ran a hand down her back, resisting the urge to dip into the waistband of her trousers. "Yes. Married. And soon."

Her brow furrowed and she said, "But, you haven't asked me."

"I haven't…oh, right, well…"

"A woman wants to be asked. You can't just assume—"

Garrett stopped her tirade with a kiss before she

worked up any steam. After a long while he stood back, took both of her hands in his, and said, "Penelope Wills, will you do me the honor of becoming my wife?"

Penny's smile was brighter than the sun, but before she could answer, another voice broke in.

"No, she will not," said Bentley from the doorway.

Garrett and Penny both turned at his voice. Now, not only did Bentley have the scratches on his face, but also an ugly scrape along his jaw. Likely, it was a memento of his run-in with Frank. His other injuries certainly were. Blood stained his torn shirt and coat, as well as the shredded left leg of his trousers. His free hand pressed against his right side. Penny could see puncture marks on the back of his hand where Frank had bitten him.

Bentley stood before them, furious yet confident, leaning slightly, favoring his right leg.

Bentley had retrieved his gun from Cotter, the one he lost to Penny, and then Penny lost to Cotter. Garrett silently cursed himself for simply tossing the gun away after he knocked Cotter unconscious and secured his hands behind his back. He'd been so anxious to get to Penny, his mind wasn't working the way it should. Now Bentley pointed a gun right at them. Garrett moved to put Penny behind him.

"Stop," Bentley said. "Or I'll shoot her first."

Bentley stepped all the way in and closed the door behind him. Frank hunched his shoulders and growled.

"Shut that dog up, or I'll shoot him in the head."

Penny bent over to sooth Frank. The dog quieted but kept his eyes on Bentley.

Bentley pointed the gun at Penny but looked at Garrett. "Toss your gun on the floor over there.

Slowly."

With great reluctance, Garrett did as instructed.

"The posse from Mill's Creek is all over this town," Garrett bluffed. "As it stands, you haven't personally killed anyone. You could save yourself from the gallows by turning yourself in."

"Nice try, Kincaid. I know for a fact most of those fools headed back to town with Sheriff McElroy. That idiot will be lucky if he still has a job after this debacle. The men who are still out looking for Cotter are far from here. Now sit down on the floor, both of you. And then scoot back against the wall. Yes, that's right."

"That's what Zeke Cotter meant when he said we'd have some time together," Penny said as she scratched Frank behind the ears. "You planned on meeting him here all along."

"I picked out this place weeks ago." He looked down at Penny, first with sadness, then with anger. "You couldn't just leave well enough alone."

"Well enough, as in married to you?"

"Like you could do better."

"She could do better with the town drunk," Garrett said, drawing Bentley's attention away from Penny.

Bentley's face tightened, reddening his skin from the neck up. He turned the gun toward Garrett. "I should shoot you first."

"No!" Penny shouted, springing to her feet. Frank stood beside her.

"Don't tell me you actually care for this...this servant of the courts." Bentley sneered.

Penny's chin lifted. "Garrett is a good and decent man. He's brave and smart and on your best day, you're not fit to polish his boots."

When Bentley looked as though he would strike her, Garrett said, "Funny thing is, if you hadn't panicked and gone after Cotter, you might have gotten away with it. Even if he confessed, you could have claimed he was lying, using you as a scapegoat. There was no proof. It would have been your word against his, a fine upstanding citizen against a known outlaw." He tugged on Penny's pant leg until she sat back down.

"I didn't panic," Bentley scoffed. "The plan all along was to meet him here. I did everything right. That clod out there couldn't even keep his face covered, couldn't follow the simplest of instructions. He was supposed to take the money from the safe. I told him he could keep half of it. I think that fool was more excited about killing than he was about the money. The idiot wanted to use his knife. I actually had to promise to pay him extra to use a gun."

Garret felt more than saw Penny stiffen beside him. His mind worked at a furious pace, trying to figure a way to overtake Bentley that didn't put Penny in danger.

"I still can't believe he left all that money just sitting there," Bentley continued.

"Going to make it harder to pay off your gambling debts," Garrett said.

Bentley paled for a moment before crimson anger claimed his expression. "How do you know about that?"

"I didn't until just now. It was a guess. I'm right, though, aren't I? I know you didn't do it for love. You don't love Penny. You had a good job, a decent life. As far as I know there haven't been any investigations into bank fraud."

"I am not an embezzler," Bentley said, raising his chin, as if stealing was somehow worse than murder.

"You don't strike me as a man with enough backbone to be that greedy," Garrett continued. That is, unless you were desperate."

Bentley reddened further. He stretched his gun-holding hand toward Garrett.

"Don't you dare shoot him!" Penny shouted.

Bentley then swung his arm so the gun pointed at her.

"Gambling debts will do that to a man, especially if they're big enough," Garrett said, goading him.

"Bunch of cheats," Bentley muttered. He deflated a little before he focused again and aimed the gun at Garrett's chest.

"We're too close to town," Garrett told him. "People will hear a gunshot. They'll certainly hear four."

"Good try, but I thought of that when I chose this place to meet that imbecile outlaw. You don't think I'd actually let him keep the money, or risk him blackmailing me, or shooting his mouth off. No, we're far enough back and up the hill. People will hear the shots, but no one will know where they came from. Not until they find your bodies, and that won't be for a while. As you can tell, this old shack isn't used for anything anymore."

To Garrett, Bentley said, "Drag Cotter back in here." He pointed the gun at Penny's head. "Move slowly, and don't try anything."

Garrett stepped out just far enough so he could take hold of Cotter's feet and drag him back inside the shack. He'd already cuffed the outlaw's hands behind his back, not that it mattered. He was still out cold.

"Make sure he's in far enough so the door will close," Bentley said, watching the marshal with a careful eye while keeping the gun pointed in Penny's direction. Cotter was only halfway in when Bentley had to step back to make room. He stumbled on his sore leg, cursed, almost fell, but caught himself in time.

"Bentley," Penny said.

Having been distracted for just a moment, he turned back toward Penny, and to his surprise, she had gotten to her feet. Before he could tell her to sit back down, before he could even raise the gun, she threw a handful of dirt into his face. He cried out his fury, dropping the gun as he grabbed for his eyes. Garrett snatched up the gun as Penny began kicking Bentley with all she had. When Bentley bent over to protect himself, she was on him.

Penny threw herself at him with such force they both hit the wall of the shack before falling to the ground. Garrett held onto Frank, who was snarling and barking, making every effort to get to Bentley. As long as she continued to be the dominant force, Garrett would let her have this.

While Bentley was bigger and stronger, the dirt made a direct hit into his eyes and blinded him. That, and the unexpected surprise of the attack, gave Penny the advantage. She knelt atop him, her knees pressing into his stomach, and pounded at Bentley's face and upper body as hard as she could with both fists while screaming her rage. Bentley begged her to stop, kept shouting her name, but he might as well have been whispering, for all she could hear over the great release of her rage and grief.

Not until she'd spent her anger, not until her words fell into sobs and her tired fists landed on the back of Bentley's protecting hands with light thuds, did Garrett let go of Frank and lift her from Bentley. The man was breathing hard and crying through the blood running from his nose and his mouth. Once Penny was off him, he curled up into a ball on his side, whimpering about needing a doctor. Frank stood guard beside him, fully attentive, ready to pounce if needed.

Garrett used the discarded ropes to secure Bentley's hands behind his back before wrapping his arms around Penny. She wept against his chest while he held her close. When her sobs turned to hiccups, he kissed the top of her head and held her some more.

Chapter 13

The wedding had been a grand affair, surprisingly, since they'd only had three days to put it together. That was as long as Garrett was willing to wait. Actually, he wanted to be married back in West Bend and claim Penny for his wife as soon as the local sheriff came to help him put Zeke Cotter and Bentley Werner behind bars. Once the ordeal in the shack was over, Penny was anxious, too, to start their new life together. But she deserved a real wedding, and she was going to have it.

The entire town, it seemed, pitched in to help. Pearl took charge of organizing the food, and Coleen O'Conner sewed nonstop making Penny's dress. Everyone came to celebrate with them. After the tragedy of the robbery and murder, the people of Mill's Creek were anxious for the happy occasion. There'd been lots of dancing in the airy barn to the music of three fiddlers. There was enough food to feed the entire town for a couple of days, and so many well wishes both Garrett and Penny had aching faces from all the smiling.

After a time, Garrett decided he had waited long enough. He ushered Penny to the door and told her everyone was having such a good time no one would notice if they slipped away. Penny didn't believe that for a minute, but she pretended she did.

On the moonlit stroll back to Penny's house, now

their home, they held hands, smiling more than speaking, Frank trotting along beside them. Once inside, the dog hopped up on the sofa and made himself comfortable. Neither Garret nor Penny would ever think to forbid him.

It took them nearly twenty minutes to get from the front door of the house to the threshold of the upstairs room because they kept stopping for just one more kiss. Once inside Penny's bedroom, an awkward silence arose.

Garrett glanced around the room. Frilly lace everywhere. Pink and yellow everything. He picked up a stuffed rag doll resting against the pink pillows on her bed. After a moment, he set it on the chair at her dressing table. It was the only chair in the room, and it looked too delicate to hold his weight.

"We'll redecorate," Penny said, smiling at the incongruity of this large, powerful man standing in her girlish bedroom. In his fine suit, he cut quite a figure. The dark finery made him look even more masculine, something she'd not thought possible. He was the finest man she'd ever seen. And now, he was her husband.

"Glad to hear that's something I won't have to fight for," Garrett answered, turning his gaze from the feminine room to his beautiful wife.

His wife. The title went through his mind for the millionth time since they'd spoken their vows. She was lovely, in her simple white gown with tiny, pink roses embroidered on the billowing skirt. Her lace veil now hung down her back, laid over the golden waves of her hair. She was the most feminine, most magnificent sight he'd ever seen. And she was all his.

Over the last few hours, they'd laughed and

socialized and danced and danced. He wasn't even close to tired. Penny wasn't either, he saw. But she had gone suddenly shy.

He watched as she opened a drawer and lifted out a fresh nightgown. He was about to tell her she wouldn't need that tonight, but as she closed the drawer, he saw the slight tremble in her hand betraying her nervousness. She didn't move then. She just stood there, clutching her nightgown to her chest.

"You know," he said. "I don't even remember if we closed the front door. I'd better go check before we end up with a kitchen full of raccoons."

It turned out to be the right thing to say. That was clear by her exhalation of relief at having the privacy to change. Besides, it would give him time to cool down. He wouldn't rush her. He wanted her more than he'd ever wanted a woman in his life, but she needed to ease into things here, no matter how difficult that was going to be for him.

When Garrett walked back into the bedroom, Penny was turning down the bed, dressed in a prim, white nightgown tied all the way to her throat with a thin, white ribbon. Her hair was loose and down around her shoulders. It flowed in a rippling river of sunshine nearly to her waist. She looked so innocent and beautiful, and nervous. She fidgeted with the sheet, smoothing out nonexistent wrinkles.

Garrett looked around the room, trying to think of something to say. She'd turned the lamp light down low. If he had his way, the light would be up all the way. He'd waited too long to see her. He settled with turning it up just a little.

She turned from the bed and clasped her hands

before her, eyes cast toward her bare toes. She seemed about to say something, but then didn't.

"Penny?"

She lifted her head to face him, opened her mouth, and then looked down again. A moment later, she raised worried eyes as high as his chin.

"Talk to me Penny?" he said in his most gentle tone.

Meeting his patient gaze, she said, "My mother died when I was seven."

"Yes, you told me."

"Pearl's been wonderful, but she raised two boys and I think sometimes she just wasn't sure what to do with me. I think she wanted to talk to me, but we just never had the chance. You know how busy these past days have been."

"Yes, I know."

"Coleen, too. During the last two fittings for my dress, she tried to talk to me, you know, privately. But both times we were interrupted before, you know…um."

He had a good idea what she was trying to say.

"What I mean is…"

"It's all right Penny," he said.

"Garrett, it's just that, well, I'm not exactly sure how…how I'm supposed to go about things, you know, tonight."

She was kneading her hands together, and as much as Garrett wanted to cross the room and take her in his arms, he worried such a move would only cause her further distress. Instead, he lifted his arms and held them open for her, waiting patiently until his new bride was ready to come to him.

Penny waited, too, trying to steady her breath and calm her pounding heart. When she finally did walk into the circle of his arms, Garrett kissed her slow and tender, as if they had the rest of their lives to stand there and share that kiss.

When after a long time he drew back, Garrett brushed her delicate jaw with the pad of his big thumb. "Don't worry, Penny." He smiled at her. "I know how to go about things."

She returned his smile, relaxing a little in his arms. Then she said, "I don't want you to be disappointed.

"You've made me feel many things in the time we've known each other, Penny. Disappointment was never one of them."

When he kissed her next, he let his passion flow a little more. Soon after, hers matched his pace. When he moved to kiss her neck, she tilted her head back to give him access. She would deny him nothing. He was her husband, handsome and strong, heroic and sensual. Her hands clung to his broad shoulders. He took her lips again as both of his hands slid down her sides until they were just below her hips.

Gathering up handfuls of her nightgown, he said in a voice turned husky, "I want to see you, Penny. All of you."

She may have moaned her answer, or maybe she was getting too lost in her own passion to have heard him. It didn't matter. For when he lifted her nightgown, she did not object, until after he'd tugged the thin garment over her head.

Suddenly realizing she was completely naked, Penny gasped and grabbed the nightgown from his hand.

"I don't have anything on," she whispered, her voice frantic, as if telling an urgent secret.

Garrett tossed the garment across the room where it landed in a quiet heap. He took one of her hands to his lips and placed a gentle kiss to her palm before saying, "I know this is all strange to you, but you'll get used to it. You're so beautiful, Penny. Please, let me look at you."

She raised her chin, and then, emboldened by his ardent plea, by the longing in his eyes, took a step back.

Garrett stood in awe of his perfect wife. Her breasts were larger than what he'd thought, creamy skin, rosy tips that both expressed and stirred desire. His palms grasped her narrow waist while his long fingers rested on the swell of her hips and his gaze strayed to her pale nest of curls at the apex of her long, lean legs. The sight of her like this enflamed his entire body with demanding desire.

Garrett bent his head, then, and pressed a soft kiss to the top of her breast. He had to taste her. He *had* to. He dragged his mouth until her sweet tip lay firm against his tongue. Her hands clung to his shoulders, slender fingers digging in as she arched up for more. He turned his attentions to her other breast for a long while, letting his hand rove from her hip to her bottom, lifting her against him in a motion that made them both senseless with desire. Garrett stood then and scooped her up into his arms.

Penny felt a chill brush over the dampness where his mouth had been. For a moment, the world tilted, and then she was on her bed. She watched as her beautiful husband removed his jacket and then unbuttoned his shirt. Bared from the waist up, Penny could now see up close what she'd only been able to admire from a distance that day at the creek. Course dark hairs over muscle narrowed at his belly and dipped into his trousers. The sight of him stole the breath from her lungs.

He bent to remove his boots and socks, and Penny watched the play of muscles across his shoulders. Such a powerful man, yet with a touch both gentle and loving. She wanted this, wanted him.

Garrett saw she was watching him with more appreciation than trepidation. Good. Her shyness was slipping away and the hungry manner in which she gazed at him now aroused him as much as any touch. He bent to kiss her, his intention to enjoy one more taste before removing the rest of his clothes. One taste of her sweet lips, however, led to another lingering taste of her breasts. Her breath caught. Her quiet mewling, an erotic cry for more, drove him the best kind of crazy.

Penny sailed upon the most wondrous waves of torment she'd ever experienced. Her entire body cried out with need of what he was giving, yet needing more, needing him to fulfill a longing she could not wholly comprehend. He brought his head up to take her mouth for another all-consuming kiss. His hand glided down her belly, leaving a fevered trail that set her skin afire. At his intimate touch, she jolted. The sensation so powerful it overwhelmed and she thought to make him stop. But she didn't want him to stop. In fact, she opened herself to him further.

Her body tensed, and her breaths heaved hard and uneven. The sensation was exhilarating, yet frightening in its intensity. Her body spiraled, all the time reaching, reaching.

"Let it happen," he whispered in her ear. And her body exploded into a million sparks.

The power of her climax plunged deep into Garrett's very soul. Never before had he known such desire, such beautiful, beckoning desire. He could wait no longer. His entire body burned to be inside of her. He wanted this woman, his wife. He wanted her *now*.

He backed away just far enough and just long enough to remove the rest of his clothing. She was still breathing hard, eyes closed, lips damp and slightly parted. When he moved atop her, he used gentle insistence to nudge her knees up so she was fully open to him. Penny opened her eyes and they found his as he braced himself above her on his elbows. Then her hand lifted to touch his face, her own expression full of wonder.

"I love you, Garrett Kincaid."

"I love you, too, Penny Kincaid."

She smiled at that, and at the hint of freshly sprouting whiskers on his jaw, but then his hardness pressed against her and her trepidation returned.

"Give me your hand, Penny," his words little more than a heavy breath he fought to control.

Once their fingers intertwined, Garrett slipped his other hand beneath her hips. He lowered himself, brushing his lips against hers. "Squeeze my hand," he whispered into her mouth. The instant she did, he pushed through her barrier.

Penny gasped at the sharp thrust of pain. She froze, waiting to see if it would pass. Only moments later, it receded and the pleasure he'd already shown her returned.

Garrett held himself perfectly still. It was killing

him, but he worried about hurting her more. He lifted up far enough to look at her face. She had her eyes closed, but no tears flowed. He bent his head again to place a kiss on each eyelid.

"Penny," he said in a rough whisper. "Are you all right?"

A small moan escaped her slightly parted lips. She opened her eyes and at his worried frown said, "It doesn't hurt anymore."

She then squirmed beneath him, showing him with her body what she wanted. At first, his movements were slow; as he wanted to be sure she was ready for more. Soon she was moving with him. He helped her find their rhythm until they reached their wondrous peaks together.

Chapter 14

"You look good behind that desk," Penny said from the open door of the sheriff's office.

She walked in, a sheaf of papers clutched in her hand. Frank trotted inside. After going behind the desk for his mandatory pat, the dog took a drink of fresh water from the bowl against the wall Garrett always left out for him.

"Frank and I were just putting these up around town," she said, turning the papers so he could see they were for the women's meeting she was organizing.

"I think you'll have a good turnout," Garrett said as he turned his smile from the dog back to his wife. And his heart swelled.

They'd only been married for eight days, yet Garrett had a gut feeling she was already carrying his child. Maybe it was just hopeful thinking. No one could know such a thing so soon. But after the frequency with which they'd enjoyed loving each other over the past week, it was certainly possible. The thought gave him a burst of excitement so strong he couldn't hold himself still.

Garrett stood and circled the desk just as Penny set down her papers. He took in his lovely wife. Dressed all in lavender, she looked like a spring flower. They'd burned her boy's clothes in the fireplace the day after the wedding. Penny said she'd had enough of those garments. Garrett was glad. While he would have made no effort to force her to rid the world of that awful getup, he was immensely happy she did.

He walked around to the front of his desk, and they were kissing before their arms had come fully around one another.

"Yes, I think being sheriff here will suit me just fine."

He meant that, too. The trade-off weighed in his favor. He'd still ride off, occasionally, if an outlaw happened to be in his area. That would be enough excitement to suit him. After that day in the shack, frankly, he'd had enough danger to last him a lifetime. Yes, he was content to maintain the town of Mill's Creek and its surroundings during the day and spend his nights in a warm bed beside his loving wife.

Penny glanced down at the papers sitting on his desk beside hers, the work he'd been doing when she'd walked in.

"Will they hang?" she asked.

"That's for a judge to decide. First, a jury has to convict them, which, with all of the evidence, I'm sure they will. You'll have to testify, Penny."

"I know. If you're worried about me, don't be. I'll do just fine."

"I know you will," he said, but he still hated to put her through that.

"You never did tell me, why did Sheriff McElroy leave?"

"He decided the law business was not for him after all. He moved back east to work in his father's haberdashery."

McElroy "decided" after Garrett suggested he

would be taken to task for his ineptitude. If he chose to leave, however, he'd leave with his dignity. McElroy muttered something about being tired of small town life anyway. He was gone the next day.

"Hmm, funny, but you know I can actually picture him selling men's clothing." She then touched the sheriff's badge pinned to the front of his shirt. "I'm glad you took the job."

"It's a good job," he said, drawing her close for another kiss. His hand couldn't resist cupping her breast.

"Garrett! Someone could walk in!"

"So what? You're my wife now."

With a giggle, she stepped away from him, slapping his hand in a playful manner. Penny leaned back against his desk. "You're sure you're not going to miss the traveling, the adventures?"

"Days of hard riding, nights sleeping on the cold, hard ground, alone, eating whatever grub I could find or had stuffed into my saddlebags? It was an adventure for a few years, but no, I won't miss it at all. Now, being away from you for weeks at a time, well, that's more missing than I'm equipped to handle."

Penny's smile broadened as she flung herself back to her husband's arms and kissed him again.

"Good," she said when their lips finally parted. "I was a little worried you'd get bored."

He laughed out loud. "With you for my wife? I think I'll be begging for bored."

As if to concur, Frank barked once, and then he barked again. Both Garrett and Penny were smiling as their lips met in a kiss.

A word from the author...

I lived most of my life in the fun city of Las Vegas. For ten years my husband and I spent several months a year traveling the country in an RV and I was fortunate enough to see every state in this marvelous country. Then we moved to the beautiful state of Michigan, where I learned about layering clothes and that boats don't have brakes.